SOLO

SOLO

First published in 2025 by Little Island Books, New Work Junction,
11 Wynnefield Road, Rathmines, Dublin, Ireland, D06 F9C1
First published in the USA in 2025

A British Library Cataloguing in Publication record for this book is available from the British Library.

Product safety queries can be addressed to Little Island Books at the above address or info@littleisland.ie

Cover illustrations by Anna Boulogne
Cover art direction and design by Lauren O'Hara
Typesetting by Rosa Devine
Copy-edited by Isabel Dwyer
Proofread by Emma Dunne
Printed in England by CPI

Print ISBN: 978-1-915071-79-8
Ebook ISBN: 978-1-915071-93-4

Little Island has received funding to support this book from the Arts Council of Ireland / An Chomhairle Ealaíon

10 9 8 7 6 5 4 3 2 1

SOLO

Gráinne O'Brien

Note on the Text

Here are some short explanations of words and phrases used in this book which you might not be familiar with if you don't live in Ireland.

The Leaving Cert
: the final exams students in Ireland take at the end of secondary school

Leaving Cert points
: Students receive points based on the grades from their Leaving Cert exams. These points determine a student's eligibility for university courses in Ireland.

Hurling
: a traditional Irish game played with a hurl or hurley (stick) and a sliotar (ball)

Grind school
: a private school which helps students prepare for exams

The Debs
: a formal dance for students in their final year of secondary school, similar to the "prom" in the USA

J-1
: a temporary Visa which allows Irish students to spend a summer working in the USA

Féile
: festival

With love to my father, Paul,
Who always believed this would happen
Even when I didn't.

Dedication
an inscription or form of words dedicating a book to a person

This book is dedicated
To me.

Not me now.
Me then.

Sweet
Lost
Anxious
Broken-hearted
Girl.

I wish I could tell you
How hard

You laugh.

I wish I could tell you
How much

You sing.

I wish I could tell you
How loved

You are.

Solo

a performance in which a performer has no partner or associate

Percussion

the striking of one solid object with or against another with some degree of force

Knock.
Knock.
Knock.

Again.
Again.
Again.

"She's asleep."

The words whisper into
My dreams.

The voices are telling
The truth.

How was it possible that I found enough peace
To sleep?

Knock.
Knock.
Knock.

The door is pushed open and there
They are.

All four of them.

Mother. Father. Brother. Brother.

A chorus of smiling faces
Seemingly unaware

That their presence is
Unwelcome.

Chorus

a body of singers, performing as a group normally,
but not necessarily, in parts

They begin
To sing.

Happy Birthday to you! (Me)
Happy Birthday to you! (Me)
Happy Birthday, dear Daisy! (That's Me)
Happy Birthday to you! (Me)

All four stand
In the doorway

Holding their treats, waiting
Expectantly.

I know what to do.

The same thing I
Have done

Every year when I hear
This refrain.

"Oh wow", is all I am able
To say

As I feel a "smile" drag its way
Across my face.

None of us believes
It's real.

But if there is one thing I can do
It's perform.

Beat

the basic unit of time chosen by the conductor
when he or she beats time

I take my cake
And wait

To blow out the candles
And

Do what is expected
Of me.

They all deserve
That much.

This family, who only want to see
Me smile.

Who only want the best
For me.

I close my eyes and the
Wish

Has slipped out and I am
Furious

With myself that I wasted
My first

Adult wish
On him.

Eighteen years of age

An adult.
At last.

Rest

silence

It's been my birthday
For ten hours

My phone is
A traitor.

Silence stalks the
Well wishes

None of which are from
Him.

Family and acquaintances
And choir members

Are kind enough to
Pay attention

To their own phones informing
Them.

"Today is Daisy's birthday.
Wish her a Happy Birthday?"

It is impossible to forget things
Like birthdays.

I should be enjoying
This day

Revelling in the
Good wishes.

I stare at the screen and obsess
Over his silence

Funebre

gloomy

Knock.
Knock.

It's gentle.
Understanding.

My mother's face
Announces itself.

Slowly. Respectfully.

"Daisy," her voice overflows
With patience,

"Your brothers are going back
To college.

They want to celebrate
Your birthday."

And I hear what she is not saying.
It's time.

Time to get up.
Time to join them.
Time to move on.
Time to come out.
Time to let go.

Duo

a piece of music for two performers

Fiachra and Tadgh are my
Older brothers.

Twins. Born ten minutes
Apart.

Not a drop of
Pain relief

My mother likes to
Tell them

When they are being
Particularly Annoying.

I love my brothers.

They tumble through life.
Always together.

Dual beings. Friends,
Brothers, soulmates.

IIddeennttiiccaall pillars
Of strength.

They came into this world
Determined

To change it.

My brothers were born
Knowing

They were meant for
Something great.

Proof that perfect lightning can
Indeed

Strike ttwwiiccee.

They feel that anything can be
Achieved

As long as they are
together.

They did their best to include me
In their club

No one's fault that I could never be
A full member.

They love me as much as they are
Capable

Of loving another
Person

And it is only a
Fraction

Of how much they love
Each other.

My brothers live together.
And laugh together.
They joke together.

They love together.
They are together.

Solo

a performance in which the performer has no partner or associate

I arrived.

A daughter born to a house crafted
By sons.

A house of chaos, confusion
And energy.

My parents doing their best to divide
Themselves e v e n l y.

Two Two.
Four Four.

Over time, natural divides
Formed

To ensure I was not
Outnumbered.

Two against Two
One parent neutral.

No forced or dramatic
Cracks

Easily and gently eroded
By trickles

Of fights and
Make ups.

It wasn't sudden or strange
But eventually

Two against Two
Became
Two against Three.

And though we are a
Complete family

When it comes to my brothers
It is them.

And

Me.

Serio

serious

My father was a
Champion.

To the people in our town, he is
Close to a God.

A boy who played for
His parish.

A man who played for
His county.

He tells stories of last minute
Points

Scored over the bar with seconds
To spare.

Our mother saw them
All.

As his classmate.
As his girlfriend.
As his wife.

He tells us about those
Summers

He would have liked to have spent
With friends

Interrailing or
On J-1s

Instead of training and
Playing.

"Are you sure this is what
You want?"

We heard our whole lives
When we asked for

Extra study sessions (them)
Extra practice time (me)

"Are you sure this is what
You want?"

It was what we wanted
We reassured.

It was what we wanted
We insisted.

It was what we wanted
We convinced.

“Doctors?”
“Yes.”

“Musician?”
“Yes.”

“To be the best?”
“To be the best?”

“Yes. Yes.”

“Yes.”

Senza
without

I used to have a
Best friend.

I had no sisters, but I had
Shannon.

Who lived next door and walked in
Without knocking.

Her parents’ friends with
My parents.

A mess that everyone needed
To untangle

As our friendship began
To fray.

We shared
Everything.

Clothes and books.
Dreams and secrets.

She knew everything
About me

Secrets told over Polly Pockets
And McFlurrys

Sitting on walls after school
Until dusk

Talking about nothing
And everything.

That all seems a
Different life

Before I became the one to
Get a boyfriend.

Before Shannon began to whisper
About me.

And used my secrets
As ammunition.

Mesto

sad and pensive

My eyes are not looking
At my mother.

They are gazing at
My disloyal phone.

Astonished it has
Betrayed me.

"He hasn't texted you."
It is not a question.

"Has Shannon texted you?"
It is a question.

I don't need
To answer.

Sighing, my mother enters
My room

Uninvited. Cautious. Determined.

She has things she wants
To say.

But Fiachra appears
At the door.

"Leave her, Mam.
She's grand."

My mother looks back
At one

Of her perfect sons and nods
As they leave.

Lusingando

perform in a coaxing, caressing, flattering, or alluring style

David is always asked to do jobs
For teachers.

He is funny and charming
And relatable.

We started
For him

Long before we started
For me.

Long before
He littered my face with gentle kisses.

Long before
He caught my eyes and held them.

Long before
His hand brushed against mine

As he handed out Bunsen burners
Or essays

With scrawled grades and hard to read
Comments.

He came to me
One day

This quiet girl who did
Her best

To not offend
Anyone.

Who played recorder
All the time

Whose face ended up in
The local paper

For winning competitions
And prizes.

In a school, none of that
Matters.

None of that was considered
Social currency.

My music made me notable
Not popular.

I am not the only person
Who wondered

Why it was that David Maloney
Decided

I was the one he would make
His girlfriend

But he always said it started
With my music.

Tief

low, deep

When First Year began,
Shannon and I

Went in as
A ppaaiirr.

Nervous but excited to make
New friends.

Promising that no matter what
We'd stick together.

A group was formed with me always
Just outside it

Missing things like weekend
Trips to town

Or to the cinema, for practices
And performances.

I was happy to have Shannon,
And the bonus

Other girls that came
With her.

None of them
Were happy

When that tall, sallow boy,
Was spotted

Holding my hand, whispering
In my ears.

I didn't care, as long as I had
Shannon.

Hand work

referring to how the fingers cover holes to control pitch and produce various notes

My hands are not smooth
Or nice to hold.

They are not delicate. They are
Calloused.

His hands are not smooth
Or nice to hold.

His knuckles are
Bruised.

His hands strong from
Gripping

And catching a sliotar. Cuts
From impact.

None of that mattered
As we fumbled

With zips and buttons
Finding our way

Up tops.
Under bras.

Down pants. Clutching
For contact.

Finding satisfaction without going all
The way.

Until the night
We did.

Pentatonic

a musical scale containing five different tones

They say that the first time should be:

1. Magical
2. Wonderful
3. Special

4. Unforgettable
5. Life altering

What it actually is:

1. Clumsy
2. Awkward
3. Disappointing
4. Short
5. Life altering

Prima volta
the first time

In the end it wasn't
Magical.

The first time.

I thought I would look different
After

The first time.

I thought things wouldn't change
After

The first time.

I thought we could become closer
After

The first time.

I didn't think he would dump me right
After

The first time.

Three Blind Mice

an English nursery rhyme and musical round

The second time I fell
In love

Was David.

The first time was in
A classroom

With a teacher squinting
Against

The sounds of sharp
Squeals.

Doing her best to admonish
The boys

Blowing as hard as
They could.

Only interested in making
Noise.

In that room of
Messers

Of squeals and
Makeshift weapons

Of plastic instruments destined
To be discarded

At the end of
The school year

So the owners' parents would
Never again

Have to suffer through
Imperfectly played

Three
            Blind
                        Mice

With that plastic recorder
In my hand

I fell in love.
For the first time.

Sempre
always

My whole life people
Have asked:

"Why the recorder?"

The recorder is the instrument
We are

Forced to play
In school.

The instrument inflicted on
Unsuspecting parents

Dragged into their home to be
Screeched

And lost and replaced
And found again

Taught by a
Teacher

Who only knows
The basics.

When I blew into
My recorder

The first time
The sound

Washed through
Me.

I placed my fingers
Lightly over

The different holes, thrilled
I could

Produce a different kind
Of sound

Just by moving
My fingers.

My parents, wanting to
Encourage this,

Tried to guide me towards
What they

Considered more impressive
Instruments.

They did not know where
To start

Encouraging a child who became
Captivated

By something as mundane
As the recorder.

A child who had become
Consumed

With a second-hand instrument
Hastily cleaned off

Having been rescued
From under a bed

Hidden by one of her
Disinterested brothers.

Wind instrument

a musical instrument in which sound is produced by the vibration of air, typically by the player blowing into the instrument

There are many different kinds
Of recorder.

Different sizes.
Different tones.

The player needs
To understand

Why that recorder was chosen
By its composer

I was not born
A natural

I do not have
Perfect pitch

I could not hear
The notes

When I looked
At them.

I am the kind of musician
That is built

Through determination and
Practice

Nothing else
Mattered.

I competed because I wanted to perform.
I studied for my exams because I wanted to perform.
I took part in chamber groups because I wanted
to perform.
I performed because I wanted to perform.

Mehr

more

My life has been about
Two exams.

The Leaving Cert
And the Grade Eight.

When your intention is to spend
Your life

Moving between notes
And staffs

It is hard to care about things
Like Maths and Irish.

All I cared about was
The Grade Eight.

Once you complete your music exams
There is nothing else to do

Nothing else to achieve
Nothing else to study for.

Once I had reached this
Final goal

I could relax and just enjoy
The music.

Leaving Cert Music should have
Been easy

To a musician like me
To a player like me
To a performer like me.

Lip fatigue

a common sensation for players of woodwind instruments due to the physical demands of playing

My lips are not soft.
They are formed

Around plastic and wood.
They crack and bleed.

They were kissable
To him.

His lips are not soft.
They are formed

By the elements, dry
And cracked

From elbows, bruised
And plump.

They were kissable
To me.

Minim

in most common time signatures, a minim is typically equivalent to two beats

His eyes
My eyes
His hair
My hands
His lips
My neck
His hands
My thighs
His breath
My skin
His tongue
My tongue

Our heat
His words
My words
Can we?
Not yet
Can we?
Not yet
Can we?
Not yet.
Can we?
Yes. yes.

Gifted

a musician who demonstrates exceptional abilities or talents

We were together
A month

When he came to where I was
Practising.

Mozart, this time, for
A competition.

He kissed me on the forehead
And presented

A bracelet, clasped it on my wrist
And said,

"Now you can think of me when
You're playing."

It glistened in the light
And

Seeing it ensured
My thoughts

Would drift away
To him

Subito
suddenly

I was practising at home the night
He called.

What should have been the final
Practice

Of a long "summer's worth" of
Repetitions.

This final exam.
This final hurdle.
This final test.

I answered assuming he was calling to say I love you.
I answered assuming he was calling to say good luck.
I answered assuming he was calling to say I am proud of you.

He spoke with more confidence
And conviction

Than I had ever heard
Him have before.

He had already decided
He was done.

He was ready to
Move on.

To focus on his hurling and
His Leaving Cert.

Had he already decided
He was done

When we were together
For the first time?

I had said that I was ready
And I was ready.

I had said
Yes. Yes.

My story is not the one girls are
Warned about.

I was ready to be with
The boy

Who kissed me in the room
Where

I'd practised my recorder.
The boy

Who would leave me
Chocolate bars

In my locker when I had
A long music lesson.

I should have noticed
Before

The night of
The first time

It had been a while since gifts
And kisses

It had been a long time since that
Boy clasped

That bracelet onto
My wrist

It had been a while since that
Boy asked

Me to play
For him.

Crescendo

gradually increasing in loudness

I just called to tell you, that I realised last night, when we were talking, and you were upset, and you weren't listening, I just don't know why you can't listen, anyway, I just need to tell you, that actually, I have had a think about it, about last night when I was telling you that

I love you, and the more I think about it, the more I realise, I don't.

I don't love you anymore.

Chiaro

clear, clearly

Knock.
Knock.

This time it is not
As gentle.

More impatient
Less understanding.

My mother appears
More frazzled.

"Daisy, it's time
To get up.

We need to go
Into town

And get your last
Few bits."

The summer is
Over.

"Shower.
Let's go."

"I don't need
Anything."

My mother sighs
Exasperation

The foundation of
Her body.

"Yes, you do. It will be good
For you.

Get up.
Now."

This was not a kind
Soothing request

This was
An order

One that no sane person would
Dare disobey.

Moderato

maintain a balanced and
measured pace throughout

My family don't hate
Each other.

We watch TV together
In the evenings.

We talk about books
And games and music.

At Christmas we have dinner
And laugh.

At Easter we eat chocolate and tell
Each other

That we have eaten too much
Chocolate.

We fight.
We make up.

We say, "I'm sorry."
We say, "I love you."

Concert

a musical performance given in public

The object of the game
Was simple.

I was to be
Their maestro.

I was putting on
A show.

The dolls were to give me their
Full attention.

My parents were to be enraptured
By my talent.

My brothers were to be in awe of my
Determination.

No matter how badly
I played

Or how many tantrums
I threw

Because the teddy bear
Conductor

Was not doing his job
Correctly

The audience always played
Their part.

My performance always
Earned

A standing ovation.

Attentamente

carefully

The car is the
One place

I can never
Get away.

They think they are
Clever

Like I can't see it coming
From the moment

The wheels start to
Move.

The locks click, ensuring
Confinement

And now the talk
Begins.

There is nowhere
To go

It is just us in
Our world

Of mother
And daughter.

"Daisy,"
She starts,

"I want you to know,"
She says,

"Your father and I understand
How hard

The last few weeks have been
For you."

Her voice breaks
A little

Is she remembering something
About her own life?

Of loves she had in a time
That existed

Before my father and my brothers
And me?

"I want you to know that we are fine
With whatever

You want to do but we
Are concerned.

Would you like to move
Into the grind school?

We thought it might be
Helpful.

Start in a new place.
A new school.

You can focus
On yourself."

Irritation clashes with betrayal at
The image

Of those whispered exchanges
The late

Nights they have spent talking
About me.

"You're worried about
The Leaving Cert –

That I am going to allow this
To fuck it all up."

Even though she is
Quite forgiving

My mother will not
Forgive this.

"Please don't curse"
And her voice

Is sharp and she seems to
Regret it.

And I regret making her
Regret anything.

"We just want you to be
Happy."

Fresco
fresh

A new start
A fresh start

A place where not everyone
Will know

Every aspect
Of my life

I try to imagine what that would
Feel like.

A new school with students
Only learning.

Living and breathing
To study.

That military place
That only exists

To grind its students down.
For one purpose.

Get as many points as possible
No matter the cost.

To their life.
To their sanity.

Laborioso

performed with a sense of industriousness,
diligence or effort

In a grind school nothing matters
But work.

There is no art
No music.

A school that is
Cold.

A school that has
No laughter.

"There is no music,"
I say.

My mother sighs and
Says nothing

Because my mother is not
Cruel or vengeful.

She is practical and considerate
Of other people.

She always finds the good
In other people.

My mother will not say

"You have not practised in months."
"You have wasted your talent for months."
"You have wasted our investment in your future."
"All you cared about was him."

She could say it
If she wanted.

I would not be able
To defend it.

My mother says,
"We can figure that out if you want us to."

"If you want us to."

The implication sits heavy
Between us.

My parents have considered that I
May never
Play Again.

"No."

And I don't say

I don't want to leave
Because of him.

Her shoulders drop
From relief

Or disappointment
It's hard to know.

"Okay,"
She says.

And that's the end
Of that.

Giocoso

lively, spirited, and joyful interpretation, reminiscent of the carefree nature associated with children

We have known each other
Our whole lives.

The same town.
The same school.
The same class.
The same birthday parties.

Standing bored as our mothers make
Polite small talk

At the same school gates.

Waiting for older siblings to make their
Chaotic appearance

And complete the family before
The drive home.

We all began to
Grow up.

Bodies and tempers and
Urges changed.

He was there on the first day
Of school.

When I clung to my mother's hand
And cried.

When I made a mistake during my first school
performance
And cried.

When a teacher clumsily tried
To explain

To our whole class what
Sex was.

I never noticed
Never saw
Never cared.

Obsessed with books and cats
And ponies

And friends and brothers
And music.

He was obsessed with soldiers
And Lego

And friends and sisters
And hurling.

We were too busy growing
And learning,

Becoming people,
To notice

Or care who existed outside
Our worlds.

Octet

an ensemble of eight instruments or voices,
or music written for it

Daisy's dad's eight rules for winning at anything:

1. You must want it
2. You really must want it
3. You must work hard
4. You must have fun
5. You must visualise the win every day
6. You must practise more
7. You must want it more
8. You must love it more

Than anyone else.

Con brio
with spirit

Before him:

Saturdays were about
My dad's rules

And rehearsals.
And rituals.

Saturdays were about
My dad's advice

And theory.
And composition.

Saturdays were about
My dad's recommendations

And practice.
And performing.

After him:

Saturdays became about shivering
On the sidelines

Of county matches
Pretending

Not to notice that he was
On the bench

Until the very last
Minute.

Thinking of what I would do
The next weekend.

Lost in his dreams
Neglecting my own.

Affettuoso
affectionate, tender

It was in the middle of the
School day

But no one was looking
For us.

No one cares where you go when you are in
Fifth Year.

It is meant to be a time of
Less pressure, expectations.

As we consider what we want
To be

When we GROW UP.

At every spare moment I would
Practise.

The sound of my recorder floating
Down the halls.

Teachers would stick their
Heads in

To enquire if I had permission
To be there.

Lingering.
To listen.

The door opened
And it was him.

Asking if he could sit.
Asking if he could listen.
Asking what I was playing.
Asking what I was practising for.
My hands getting hotter.
My face getting redder.
My heart beating faster.

Every question accompanied by a
Step forward.

Towards my body.
Towards my face.
Towards my lips.

Until his were on mine.

I got my first proper
Kiss.

While I was holding
My recorder.

Forte

loud, strong

"Tell me how you do it,"
He'd asked

One night when I'd performed and won
Another trophy.

'I practise.' I'd smile as I went
To kiss him.

He'd pushed me back and said,
"I mean it."

And I told him.
About my father.

How he talks to me about
My visualisation.

My goals.
My habits.

How he tells me about
His visualisations.

His goals.
His habits.

I tell him about
My brothers.

How he talks to them about
Their visualisations.

Their goals.
Their habits.

And I tell him about
My mother.

Say nothing.
Do nothing.

Keep going.

"You need to want
It more."

"I do want it," he snaps.
I know

David thinks he
Wants it.

"Not enough," I say and
I know

He's surprised that I have
Said

Something critical
Of him.

"It isn't enough to
Go training.

It isn't enough to do as much as
The rest.

Some are naturally faster than you
Some are naturally more flexible than you
Some are naturally more focused than you

You can only beat them
Two ways.

You need to do more.
You need to want it more."

He became

Stronger.
Faster.
Focused.
Determined.

People noticed he
Wanted it more.

No one could believe it
Except for me.

I was the one
In his ear

Telling him how much
He could achieve

As long as he wanted
It more.

Block harmony

a succession of similar or identical chords

The heat is oppressive for August
In Ireland

Mam pushes me through
The queues

Muttering about all these people
Who have left

Back-to-school jobs
To the last minute.

We are having a nice time.
The first time ever

This job has not been tainted
By the necessary purchase

Of	Of
Two	Two
Of	Of
Every	Every
Thing	Thing
Else	Else

Étude

a composition intended for practice

My parents are not
Musical.

They know they like
Music.

But they do not know
Its mechanics.

They do not know
Its foundations.

They love music but
They can't

Count and hear and sing
The notes.

"I know it comes to you easily," my father
Would say.

"But you still need to be willing
To work hard.

You need to make sure you
Want it more."

And I did. I always
Worked hard.

To be better.
To play better.
To feel it better.
To hear it better.

I always made sure I wanted
It more.

My evenings and weekends were
Filled with lessons.

Singing lessons, theory lessons,
Recorder lessons.

Scales, repetition and
Breathing exercises.

One night a week was for
Friends or TV or reading.

The rest were for
Music.

How much noise did my parents
Endure

During those days, weeks,
Months of years

When my talent did not match
My obsession.

Mistakes repeated over and over
And over again.

I would not move on until it was
Perfect.

No matter how long
It took.

They were happy to know
Where I was.

How can you maintain your breath
If you are smoking.

How can you get up early and practise
If you are out late.

How can you go to discos if you
Are playing

In a Sunday
Morning concert.

It kept me focused.
Kept me going.

Ensured that I was a good daughter
A good girl.

I had the recorder.

It was my whole life
Until him.

I saw the worry on my parents' faces
When I entered a room

Holding David's hand and not
My recorder.

The glances they threw
Over my head

When I was sitting with him
On the couch

When I should have been sitting
A lesson.

I felt their fear, that it
Was slipping

Away all because
Of him.

I no longer cared about
performing.

My parents had opinions
I am sure

But for whatever reasons
They don't seem

To want to discuss or
Address them.

Maybe they just knew
I wouldn't listen.

Cambiare

to change, such as to a new instrument

Exam papers
Revision books
Fresh pens
Refill pads
Folders

Hardly worth the money to get
Anything else.

There is no need for a new
Schoolbag

This is the last year
Left.

The year that our lives have been
Pointing towards

Since the day I started
Secondary school.

Everything has been
For this year.

Looking towards the future
The next steps

The next phase
Of life.

The Leaving Cert is all
That should matter.

The Leaving Cert is all
I should care about.

Minaccioso

menacing

"Right," Mam says
Weary but

Encouraged that we only have one last
Stop.

"You don't need a whole new uniform
Thank goodness for that.

But you have outgrown your skirt."
She eyes me up.

"You're still growing. I wonder how tall
You will end up."

I am already taller
Than her.

We push our way into
The uniform shop.

And observe
The chaos.

"Daisy. Rebecca. How lovely
To see you."

A familiar voice
Churns my stomach

A voice that never approved of her son
Having a girlfriend

Who probably celebrated
The news

Delighted I will never again
Ring her doorbell

And slink up the stairs to her
Son's bedroom

Where we were able to do
Plenty of damage

Even with his bedroom door
Slightly ajar.

Her periodic attempts to listen in
Unnoticed.

Oblivious to how fast two people can
Pull apart

At the sound of a
Creaky floorboard.

Dissonance

clash

The tone suggests it was not
Lovely to see us

My face burns at her stare
Wishing she could have pretended

She hadn't seen us
But she is

Not the kind
Of woman

Who can't resist an opportunity
To comment.

My mother stiffens and
Exhales.

"All set for the start of the year?"
She speaks again.

My mother's face belongs
To a warrior

Ready protect her daughter against
An equal opponent.

Natural

a note which is neither flat nor sharp

I threw a tantrum once
After a féile

A local competition
I did not come first

I did not deserve to
But I thought I did.

I smacked my recorder
Into its case.

Brimming with tears of anger and
Embarrassment.

My father wasn't there
That day.

He had gone somewhere with
My brothers

And I blamed it on
That.

Because he was
Not there.

Because he left me with
My mother.

My mother was not
A champion.

She smiled and chatted as
I fumed.

Kicking at my chair
Arms folded.

Head down, eyes on
The floor.

She waited till we got
To the car.

"Daisy," she said and her tone
was even.

She didn't sound mad, but
Disappointed.

"I know your father has taught
You and the boys

Lots of different things about
How to win.

But you need to learn
How to lose."

That day she
Taught me

How to behave in front of
Other people.

Encouraging me to keep my face
Passive.

"No one needs to know what
You are thinking, Daisy.

The only person who knows you have made a
mistake is you.

The only person who needs to know you are upset
is you."

Say nothing.
Do nothing.
Keep going.

These words have stayed
With me during

Every misplayed note.
Every missed entry.
Every mistaken rhythm.

Poco a poco
little by little

"Just getting the last bits." My mother
Moves towards

The till and throws
The skirt

That very last thing we needed
On the counter.

My eyes on the harried staff member
Folding it away.

"Daisy," her voice is smooth
And careless,

Her body language the opposite
Of my mother's.

I can see as she stands
At the till

Overly impatient with
The struggling boy

Who looks familiar to me
From school.

"I am so sorry things
Didn't work out.

But sure ye are only young.
Teenage romances.

They aren't meant to last
Are they?"

Say nothing.
Do nothing.
Keep going.

"Poor David is very upset.
Very upset.

I hope this won't affect
His exams."

Say nothing.
Do nothing.
Keep going.

"And," she says with a pause, "yours,
Of course.'

My mother is pushing her way back
Towards us

I have never seen her face
So severe.

"Rebecca," his mother says turning to
Mine

Who cuts her off, before she can
Get started.

"Don't you dare speak to my daughter
Again."

Sharp

a note raised by a semitone

I don't think I have ever
Seen

My mother rude to anyone
Before.

My mother is sweet and
Caring.

She thinks about everyone.
She worries about everyone.

She cares what people think
About her.

She likes to quote
Michelle Obama,

"When they go low
We go high."

Mrs Maloney sighs,
Clearly disappointed

That my mother
Has chosen

To behave with such
Little dignity.

David was encouraged
To call

My parents their
First names.

This woman was always
"Mrs Maloney".

"Now Rebecca, there is no need for any
Unpleasantness.

We all got along before
And we can now too.

They are so young – these teenage
Dalliances never work out. Well..."

She pauses, looking my
Mother up and down,

"I suppose it did
For you.

But I can't say I am
Too sorry.

They need to focus on
Exams and friends."

My mother takes a long look
Down her nose.

"I can't say that I am
Sorry either

Since your son is such
A little prick."

Apaisé
calmed

We walked back to the car
In silence.

Back in the car she
Waits until

The doors click to
Confirm

They are locked before
She speaks again.

"Daisy, I shouldn't have
Said that.

But she needs
To understand

That David was
Lucky

You ever glanced
In his direction.

And he is a little prick for
What

He has done
To you."

She turns on
The radio.

And we drive home listening to
The sound

Of someone else's
Broken heart.

Ferne

distance, as if from a distance

He wasn't always
A prick

He was welcomed into
Our home

Always asked about
His family.

My father would sit
And chat

While I was over-preparing
For us

To be dropped
To the cinema.

They would talk about
His training

My brothers listening in
With genuine interest

They too had played once for our
Local team

Harbouring dreams of playing
For their county.

In their father's
Footsteps.

A place always offered
For dinner.

To the boy who broke
My heart.

Recorder

a simple wind instrument without keys

Finally home I thought I would
Be able to escape

Back into the confines of
My room

My father's voice
Calls me

From the kitchen
Where he has

Been waiting, probably since
Receiving

A hastily composed text
From my mother:

We need to talk
To you.

My father clears
His throat.

The emotional things aren't easy
For him

But he is trying to not make
My mother

Speak all the words of
comfort.

He averts his eyes away
From my red eyes

And looks slightly above
My forehead.

"We wanted to get you something
Special.

Eighteen is a big one. We are sorry
It is late –

We were waiting for it to be cleared
Through customs."

He mutters something
About Brexit

Because he cannot
Help himself.

He has something
Behind his back

He presents it
Proudly.

A black leather case.
A brand-new alto recorder.

I flick open the case
And lift the lid.

I know I have no right to it
But I take it.

Baroque

grand, ornate and elaborate style that
is characterised by a sense of drama, exuberance
and tension

My father is
A good man.

He is the kind of man
That works hard

To provide
For his family.

We always knew not to ask
For too much.

My father was the one who spent
His weekends

Driving me to competitions and concerts
And performances.

He would sit in the audience
Closing his eyes

As my fingers danced
Over the holes of the recorder

As my breath moved
Effortlessly.

He did not understand what
I was doing.

But he knew
That I did it well.

Better than all
The other children

On all the
Other instruments.

My brothers would complain
I got

More attention than they got
Choosing to forget

The hours I practised recorder in
The car

While my parents stood in
The cold

For their hurling matches until they
Quit playing.

We all knew neither
Of them

With their eyes focused on science
And medicine

Neither of them would be better than
The other

Neither was going to be
The best.

But I could be.

Obbligato

necessary, an accompanying part that cannot be omitted

For most people music is

A distraction
A pleasure
A pastime
An afterthought

For the car
For the gym
For walks
For runs
For parties
For pubs
For nightclubs
For dancing
For singing

Music is something I am.

Notes travel across my skin
Down my neck.
Down my back.

My spine could be
A xylophone.

Each vertebra a

d
i
f
f
e
r
e
n
t
Note.

Music informs how I walk.
How I breathe.

How I live.
Who I am.

I wasn't concerned with being
The best.

I wanted to surround myself with
A cloud
Of music.

To wrap myself in a blanket
Of crotchets
And quavers.

Scale

a sequence of notes ascending or descending stepwise

My whole life
I have found joy
In music
I can't say
For sure
When this changed
From something
I **needed** to
Do
To something
I **had** to do
A chore
A distraction
An invasion in my life
A nuisance
Something to avoid

But I think
It started
With
Him

Lacrimoso

in a tearful manner

It's a relief
To cry

About something that isn't
Him.

It is too much for my father
Who nods

His gift is given, he is now
Free to

Leave the room. My mother
Remains.

Her teenage daughter weeping
At the sight

Of a new recorder that we are all
Unsure

I will ever
Play.

My mother knows every inch of
Who I am

And who I could
Someday be.

I can tell her mind is working
Hard.

Trying to make this
Better.

Figuring out how to make the pain
Go away.

My mother lives
Her life

To that clichéd
Mantra:

"You are only as happy as your
Saddest child."

Cantata

a choral work that uses solo voices with
an instrumental accompaniment

"Daisy, we think you should
Go back to choir.

I met Aidan today, he was
Asking for you."

I bristle, yearning to
Lash out

To tell her to mind her own
Business.

A desperate need to condone
The choices

Of my past self, the girl
Who worked

So hard to damage
My present.

I want to yell

I don't want to sing.
I am done with music.
I am sick of the practice.

It has nothing to do with
Him.

Leaving choir
Giving up recorder

Losing my friends
Losing myself.

"Give yourself this, Daisy.
It will help you.

Give yourself something to
Focus on..."

An embargo on his name
Has been enforced.

"It might help you reconnect
with your music."

Choir exists outside
Of school.

It takes place in a music
Room

Above a church where we
Practise.

It is about
The group.

The sound.
The togetherness.

You don't stand out.
You blend in.

I look down at the recorder
The gift from them

That is more than a
A new instrument

It is a gesture of
Encouragement.

A hint that maybe I can find my way
Back.

To my old self and a life
Without him.

Choir

a body of singers, performing as a group

I have always treated singing
Differently

To the way I treated
The recorder.

I sing soprano, the highest
Range.

Singing in choirs was the gift
I gave myself.

There was no pressure
To learn and drill.

It was another thing I allowed
To slip away.

Missed rehearsals.
Forgotten performances.

Overtaken by the need
For dates.

A choir is not where you go if you want
To be alone.

In choirs there are no stars
Only constellations.

Sotto voce

said or sung in a quiet voice

I joined this choir three years ago,
Followed by Shannon

Who soon left it to pursue
Other things.

I stayed and carved a new
Special place

For me.

Among these singers of varying ages
And skill levels

Who join each other just
To sing.

I don't know what conversations
Took place

Between our choir's director and
My mother.

I make my way to the practice room
And remember

This place is always
Cold.

A relief in the summer.
A burden in the winter.

Concern is etched across
Aidan's face

As he greets me at the top of
The stairs.

My mother has
Spread the word.

A game of whispers.
Adult to adult.

"She's been dumped?"
"She's been dumped."

If he has wondered where I have been
He does not say.

If he wondered why I stopped coming
He does not say.

If he is disappointed in me
He does not say.

He hands me a few
Pages of music

And gestures for me
To sit down.

Further down the line than
I used to be.

I take my new seat blinking away
Tears

Ashamed that I have
Lost my place

Let down others when I lost
My voice.

Alto

a low-register voice, properly referred
to as a contralto

More members make their way into
The room.

Friendly waves and greetings
Welcome me back.

I cannot stand it.
I look around

And catch the eye of
A face

I have never
Seen before.

In the alto line. She looks
My age,

Her appearance is curious.
Nothing new

Ever happens
In this town

Where everyone stays or
Leaves.

"Welcome back!" Aidan throws out
His arms

Truly delighted to
Have his

Community choir back
Together again.

"We have said goodbye
To some members.

Off to college and
Other things.

We are delighted to welcome back
Daisy!"

I hate the kindness
Of his words

The grace
I am given

This welcome that feels warm
And genuine.

"And we have a new alto! Welcome, Flora,
All the way from Dublin."

To live here.
What a tragedy.

Jesu, der du meine Seele, BWV 78

a Canata written by Bach studied
by Irish Leaving Certificate students
as part of their Music curriculum

"This year we are doing something
Really special."

And his face is one of pure joy
And excitement

Aidan believes everything we do as a choir
Is a treat.

"We've been asked to perform
Jesu, der du meine Seele for

The local Leaving Certificate Music
students.

The performance is in April, ahead of
Exams in June.

Plenty of time
To practise.

And I know Flora and Daisy,
Our Leaving Cert students,

Will benefit
Especially."

Aidan is under the
Impression

He is giving me some kind
Of gift.

"For those of you who aren't
Lucky enough

To talk about one of Bach's most
Incredible works

For two whole years like Flora
And Daisy

This is going to be a
Wonderful chance

For us to learn more about Bach
Together."

Flora is grinning at Aidan's words
And I

Am struggling to grasp
At something

Familiar just out
Of reach

Ängstlich
anxiously

I have never dreaded going
Back to school.

I wouldn't say I am
Excited by

The possibility of work and
Drama and pressure.

Of teachers that hate you or like you
Or don't care either way.

Of classmates that care
Too much

About being there or don't care
Enough.

Of gossip and chatter
And stories

That are true or
Not true.

I managed to walk through
School life

Being seen just the right amount
To survive.

So consumed by music
And study.

Friendship with Shannon.
Relationship with David.

I didn't do enough to offend
Anyone.

Tomorrow will be about
Him

And me and what
Happened.

And whose fault
It was.

And whose fault
It wasn't.

And it will be a stage
Or a circus

A role I never auditioned for.
An audience I never asked for.

I am one of the players expected to
Know my part

And I don't know the piece because
I never practised.

March

a piece of music with a strong, regular rhythm

Once again, we are
In the car.

This time, the radio is on
Doing its best.

To distract us
Both.

I know my mother
Is concerned.

About what this day
Will look like.

Throughout the drive
She glances

To the left to look
At me.

As I gaze forward
Eyes on the road

I see the reluctant
Uniform-wearing soldiers

Marching towards school.
Begrudging their lot in life.

A summer over.
A new year begins.

I am becoming
Embarrassed

At how much I relate to songs
On the radio

Wishing I could be more
Together

Than any girl who gets emotional
Because of

The words of pop stars
They've barely heard of.

"Text me," my mother says as she gives me
Aquickkiss.

Afraid to show me too
Much affection

Knowing it can be
Social suicide.

As if that could be worse
Than

Being a nobody who was dumped
By a somebody.

Sprechgesang

a style of dramatic vocalisation intermediate between speech and song

I step forward towards
The front door.

My hand pushing the clearly
Marked pull.

The door opening because nothing is ever
Put on properly.

I pause, waiting
For a gap

In the stream of students
Marching

Hoping I can slip in between them
Unnoticed.

I hear my name and my heart
Skips, looking

For its source, aware nobody here
Could be

Excited to see
Me.

Through the throngs of students
Milling about

Hugging, chattering,
Exchanging stories

Our principal is at his office door
Wearing a new suit.

Talking to an unfamiliar
Girl.

Approaching, I realise she is not
Unfamiliar.

I have not seen her here
In our uniform.

But I have seen her across
From me.

Her amused eyes flicking
Over her music

Smiling at the enthusiam of our
Choir director

The girl who moved all the way
From Dublin.

And joined our community
Choir.

"Daisy!" our principal says, with an energy
I suspect

Will be gone by the end
Of the day.

"Can I introduce you to
Flora."

I nod, unsure as to my
Intended role.

I feel the eyes of my
Classmates burning

Into my back, failing to whisper
To each other.

I too have walked those halls
Whispering audibly

Basking in the misfortune of
Others.

Engaging in the only
Real currency

A student can
Trade in.

"Did you hear about?"

Him. And

Me.

Intro

the introductory section of a piece of music

Flora is looking at me with the same
Mischief

In her eyes that she had
At choir.

"I hope that you will show Flora
Around,"

The principal says, already turning
His back to us.

This request is not
A request.

I am relieved to spend
A few moments

With this girl who knows nothing
About me.

But unsure in this unexpected turn
Of events.

While I scramble for something to say
Flora finds it.

"I know you," she says, direct.
To the point.

"From choir." I nod
Adding nothing.

"Ah yeah." We stand there
Looking at each other.

"Should we go then?" I nod, grateful
She's taking charge.

We walk on, falling into
Step.

"Lockers are this way,"
I say.

We need to stop at
The office

And confirm that Flora's
Parents

Have paid the one hundred
Euro

Deposit that will not be
Returned

Unless the locker is left
Empty

At the end of
The year.

Walking towards the sound of
Clattering metal

I see a glimpse of what could be his
Back.

Rounding the corner I focus back
On Flora.

"You moved here? From Dublin?"
"Yeah,

My da took a job at the university
Lecturing."

"Cool." I don't know
What else to say.

"S'not really." And I suppose she
Is right.

It probably isn't cool to leave your home
And your friends.
And your choir.
And your school.

"What does he lecture in?" I ask, to ask
Something.

"Music," she says offering
Nothing else.

And I don't feel the need to take more
Than I was given.

Scherzando
in a playful manner

I am not entirely sure
What

I should be doing with this
New person.

What would Flora need
To see?

Here are the bathrooms that you can go to
If you want

To hide from everyone or cry
In peace.

Behind the art room is where
Students go

To ditch and smoke – I have never been
Invited there.

Nor would I want
To be.

Here are the lockers.
Here are the benches.

Here is the canteen.
Here is the tuck shop.

Places that every school
Has that

Can hardly be considered
Extraordinary.

I think of something.
"What's your locker number?"

"Seventy-eight." She grins
Then frowns.

My locker is number two hundred and
Seven.

I point Flora in the direction
Of hers.

And walk away towards
My own.

Pulling it open and
Shoving in

All the tools needed for
A Leaving Cert student

To ensure
Her success.

Other students jostle around me, and
I close the door

Taking a little too long to slip on
My new padlock.

Not sure I can turn around
And face the day.

Flora appears at my side
Again

"Let's go this way,"
She exclaims

Pointing down the corridor that
Has

The most amount
Of students.

Risoluto

energetic

I can already tell:
Flora

Is a girl who knows
What she wants.

"Do you have your timetable?"
I ask

Pulling out my own colour-coordinated
Page.

Meticulously put together by
Our school secretary

Provided to our parents via
Email.

Telling us where and when we
Need to be.

"Let's not bother with that," Flora says,
"It's the first day."

The idea of not going to
Classes

And the horror it
Presents me with

Has clearly made its way across
My face

And into Flora's
Mischievous eyes.

She smiles and pulls out her
Timetable.

Holding them together
For comparison.

Biology
Home Ec
Maths (OL)
Irish (OL)
Music
English
French

"They are the same,"
Flora says

With what feels like
Genuine delight.

She loops her arm
Through mine

And with a nod
Of her head

Instructs me to direct her where
We need to go.

Allegro
cheerful, bright

The refreshing distraction
Of Flora

Begins to suck away as we
Weave

Through the sea of
Students.

Flora appears oblivious to
The curious glances

Her unfamiliar face is drawing
From students

Who have no idea how
To comprehend

The presence of someone new
Among them.

Double takes become
Open gawping

Stares when they realise who
She is with.

My classmates are not used to seeing
Me with

A person who is not
David.

A person who is not
Shannon.

"So," she asks
Her voice singsong

Her eyes gazing around taking in
The crowd

Of students downloading
Everything

They need to know about
Their summers.

"Who do you hang out with?"
Flora asks.

The question is so simple and
So complicated.

The truth slips out before I can
Catch it.

"No one."
No one.

Flora nods at this answer
Her simple acceptance

A relief and
An annoyance.

Tremolo

a wavering effect in a musical tone

He is there in front of me
My ears begin to throb

My hands begin to sweat
I start to shake

New pants.
Old jumper.

A flash in my mind of the
Countless times

I wore that jumper when
I was cold.

Or just wanted the smell of him
Around me.

The thought dances into my
Traitorous mind

That he could have been the one to refuse
The purchase of

A new one so that he could be
Reminded

Of the times when I would
Wear it.

Cupo

dark, sombre

Say nothing.
Do nothing.
Keep going.

If it's going to happen it is going to happen
Now.

This place is where it
Began.

And as our eyes connect, I see his eyes flick
Towards Flora

As curious as the rest of them
Wondering who is

This new student
This unknown creature

But he nods his head and keeps
Walking.

The nod says
Yes. I see you.

Yes. It's over.
No. There is no going back.

For him.
For me.
For us.

My brain is not communicating to
My legs

They need to keep moving
We need to keep moving

Don't stop, please
Don't stop.

"So, who is that then?"
Flora's voice.

"No one," I reply.
"Ah," Flora says. "I see.

"Right," she continues into my ear.
"Where are we going?"

She pulls at my arm, tugging me
Away from

This moment I have been
Hoping for.

The moment I have been
Focused on.

The moment that is the reason
I came back here.

The moment that for weeks
I have been

Dreading and anticipating dismissed
With a nod.

And Flora and I simply move on
Arm in arm

Towards Flora's first
Assembly.

Audience

a group of people who are listening

"To our new students,"
Our principal says

With his arms an unwelcome gesture
Of welcome

Appearing to take in the looks of fear
And anticipation

From the First Years, and apathy
From everyone else.

I'm looking at their fresh uniforms
And

How small they
All are.

It seems impossible that
I could

Have ever been
That young.

That excited to be welcomed
To school.

"And of course
Welcome back."

He gestures around to the rest
Of us

Though we are well aware that
For him

Some of us are not
Welcome back.

"I hope you all had a lovely relaxing
Summer."

The teachers are lined up
Against the wall.

Some look as thrilled as us
To be back.

"We know that this year will be tricky
For some of you,"

He says, gesturing towards
Where

The Third Years and Sixth Years
Are sitting

Doing their best on this first
Day back

To not think about
Looming deadlines

And state exams.

There are the usual housekeeping
Details

That no one is listening to,
Except for those

Wide-eyed First Years who have never
Heard them before.

Beside me, Flora is looking on,
The attention

She's paying is half,
At best.

"And finally," he says just
At the moment

When those of us who sense
The ending

Is due are beginning to shuffle
Around

Squeaking shoes against
The hard

Wooden floor that is scuffed
By decades

Of cheap shoes that rarely fit
Properly.

"We have some exciting news
To share:

Congratulations to David Maloney and
Gareth O'Dwyer,

Who helped their local Under-
Eighteens team

Win the county final for their club
Just last week."

Applause. Applause Applause.

A champion.
At last.

Say nothing.
Do nothing.
Keep going.

Fort

onward

"We are hopeful that with these
Fine young men

On our team this will be the year
We are able

To break The Curse."
This is something

I learned about GAA when I was
With David.

There is always some kind
Of Curse.

A supernatural thing has
Happened

That explains away why a
Team

That believes it should be winning
Isn't winning.

Our school has not won the Byrne
Cup in over thirty years.

Every year the students talk about
The Curse

More than we talk about
Anything else.

My father doesn't believe
In curses.

Play harder.
Work harder.
Train harder.

Want it more.

Than all the rest of them.

Amarevole

with bitterness

I see a girl leaning over
To whisper to him

A little too close
A little too gently
Hair flicked

The girl who used to be
My friend.

The girl with whom I learned
About animals

And boy bands
And tampons.

Shannon, more than
Anything

Wanted to be part of
The crowd.

She is laughing and flicking
Her hair

At whatever David and Gareth
Are saying.

Glancing in my direction,
Lingering on Flora

Giving her the same
Curious glances

That she is getting from
Everyone else.

Her hair is longer than I have
Ever seen it.

"You can see that girl's extension glue
From here,"

Flora murmurs in my ear and
I snort,

And immediately feel
Guilty.

I don't speak badly about Shannon
To other people.

This feels like the ultimate
Betrayal.

But Flora is right.
Shannon's hair

Is made of something
Fake.

We are dismissed and
Rising to our feet

I can catch a glimpse of Shannon
Evidently fascinated

By a retelling of a match
In a way

She certainly wasn't when she
She was snippily refusing

To come and keep me company
On the sidelines.

Arraché

torn, a forceful pizzicato

In the last few years, I noticed
That Shannon

Likes to blame me
For things.

She does it in a way that makes
It hard

TO CONFRONT.

Death by a thousand cuts
And comments

Muttered under her breath.
Not what

She says but how
She says it.

She says I should be more
Considerate

Of her feelings when I am
Achieving things.

That I should have thought
About how

It would make her feel
When I got

That award
That concert
That standing ovation
That acknowledgement
That boyfriend.

I don't know how to
Defend myself

Against these accusations
That she manages

To make sound almost
Reasonable.

And now there she is
With them and him

Instead of here
With me.

Imperioso

overbearing

I overheard them, a day
Right before

The summer holidays officially
Began.

Fifth Year was over, the shadow
Of what

Lay ahead just starting to
Grow.

The gaggle of them stumbled into
The senior girls

Bathroom, laughing and joking,
Shannon's voice

The loudest. I was about to call
Out

From the cubicle where I had
Been peeing and scrolling

Enjoying the peace
That shattered

As they started

Why would he pick her?
She's a nobody really.
She's just, there, you know?

A symphony of voices articulating
Every insecurity

Led in their performance
By Shannon.

Verlierend

losing, dying away

I stayed for as long as
I could bear

Before clicking the lock
The sound

Of flushing and hand dryers
And secrets

Their faces surprised at first
Then bold.

I never texted Shannon again
And she

Never texted me.

Accelerando

moving faster

Our first day back has passed quicker
Than usual.

Flora is the real star of the
First day.

A new student who needs to be
Introduced.

And tell us all a little bit about
Herself.

For every teacher who's as bemused
As the rest of us

At the arrival of a new student
To our small school

During her Leaving Cert
Year.

"Students usually leave us
This year."

One teacher joked a nod to those
Empty chairs

That should hold our classmates of
Twelve years –

Those who decided
This school

Has taken them
Far enough

And handed their precious education
To a grind school.

I wonder what that must feel like
To teachers

Who have spent five years
Doing their best

To get us through these exams
As well-equipped

And unscathed
As possible.

For parents to say at this
Crucial point

What you are doing
For their

Precious children was
Not enough.

Letzt
last

The last class of the day
Is Music.

Neither of us really wants
To go.

I know my own reasons –
Flora's are a mystery.

"Should we ditch?"
She asks.

I want to avoid
That room, avoid

Ms Willis, who
No doubt

Would be wondering where I have
Been since

I sent that text:
I failed.

Ignoring the calls and
The concern.

In the end, she called
My mother to ask

What had happened.
What had gone wrong?

She gave up her summer
To help me prepare

Not realising how little practice
Was done

When she wasn't
There.

When we enter the room, Ms Willis
Smiles and

I think there is a new space
Between us

Bedächtig

cautious, deliberate, slow

"Flora, welcome," Ms Willis smiles,
"It's today's last class

I'll assume we all know who you are
And I won't ask you

To introduce yourself for what no doubt
Will be the sixth time

Today." Flora nods.
Ms Willis

Drops her teacher persona
And gives

Flora one of her
Real smiles.

"I know that you will be fine in your
Music exam.

Your father taught me
In college.

I am so happy to have you here
with us."

Flora's face becomes a pillar
Of ice.

Unnoticed by anyone
But me.

Redotto

reduced

"Now," Ms Willis continues
On and

And Flora's face has
Melted quickly.

She pulls out her
Copy and a pen.

This is the first time I have
Seen Flora

Engage with school
All day.

“I am afraid we need to get right
Into it.

I don’t need to repeat the lectures of
My colleagues.

Let me reassure you that
The points

For Music are just as good
As the rest.

Those of you looking to pursue a career
In Music

In the long-term, it would
Do you well

To give this subject as much time
As you can manage.”

She does not look
At me.

“Now, that’s my little spiel.
Let’s get into it.”

She walks towards the board and pulls the lid off
A whiteboard marker.

It snaps in the way only a new
Marker can.

"Your exam, as you well know,
Is split:

The theory and listening.
The composition.
The practical.

The plan for the year is very simple.

Revise.
Revise.
Revise.

Practise.
Practise.
Practise.

You know you need six practical
Pieces.

I expect you have been
Rehearsing

For the summer but humour me
As I do

This little refresh for
Those of us

Who have more cobwebs
Than others."

This time it feels like she does
Look at me.

And I feel the shame of knowing
The spiders

Have crawled over me for
The summer.

"Does anyone have any
Questions?"

I don't even know where
To start.

Accolade

brace, a line used in music to join two or more staffs carrying simultaneous parts

The bell insists
We go home.

I do my best to gather up my things
And move

From the room as quickly
As possible.

"Daisy." She calls me after me.

Of course she does.

Ms Willis is a kind, considerate
Person.

She loves music as much as
I do.

She plays the saxophone
And sings.

She has been invested in
My future

Invested in my talent
Invested in my music
Invested in me.

Flora has questions in
Her eyes

Wondering why a teacher
Would want

To speak to me
In private

On our very first
Day back.

Curious glances from the rest of
My classmates

As I stand, shifting my weight from
Foot to foot

Needing to be on my way
To my locker.

"Daisy." She says my name again as if she is
Unsure of it.

Or perhaps she thinks that I
Am unsure of it.

"I know you don't want
To talk

About everything
That happened

During the summer and I understand.
I am very sorry.

That must have been terrible
For you.

I have failed exams
Myself.

It is never a good feeling
Especially

When you've worked
So hard."

We both know I didn't work
That hard.

I don't say anything.
There isn't anything to say.

"I have some concerns,"
She says,

And she is not being
Unkind.

"I am not sure what your plans are
For your practical.

But I think it would be a
Good idea

To play some of the pieces you are more
Familiar with

Than the ones you were focusing on
This summer."

I focused on nothing but him
This summer.

"It's the first day," I say, since I can't
Think of anything else.

"You and Flora are the
Only ones

On my list that have
A question mark.

For her, of course,
It's expected."

It isn't expected for me.
It is a disappointment for me.

"Have you given it any thought?"
She asks.

"I've had a lot going on," I say, repulsed by my
Misery.

Clam

slang for a wrong or misplaced note

She nods as if she
Understands.

"I have been thinking about you.
These are

Some of my favourite pieces
You've played.

Any of these
Played perfectly

Could get you
The best result."

This list is prepared in her
Lovely handwriting

Proof that she really has
Been thinking

About me during
Her summer

When I was
Busy

Ignoring her calls.
Licking my wounds.

"These are Grade Five pieces," I say looking at
The list.

Of what she thinks I am
Capable of.

Her face tightens. "My job is to get you
The best result, Daisy.

These pieces are stunning, you play them
Beautifully.

This isn't like..." She hesitates and continues.
"The Grade Eight."

That failure hangs
Between us.

"The Leaving Cert practical is not about playing
The most complicated piece.

It's about performing, and
Performing well.

And you can do that with
Grade Five pieces."

Semplice
simply

Music lingers in my bones.
My insides.

My skin hums in tune with the notes
That I play.

I don't think about
Music.

I don't think about
Breathing.

I don't consider
Music.

I don't consider
Walking.

I don't worry about
Music.

I don't worry about
Existing.

Music has always been there
The same way

My hair has always been attached
To my head.

The same way my reflection is exactly
What I expected it to be.

Music is not something that I do.
Music is something that I am.

It forms the very fabric of who I am
As a person.

At least...

It used to.

Strolling

a relaxed and leisurely walking tempo

"Right," said Flora, as I stood next to
Her locker

Watching her shove all her books
Into it.

She doesn't intend to
Bring any

Of her books home for
The night.

My bag is heavy on my back
And I

Feel embarrassed to be taking
Books home,

Knowing that I will spend the night
Crying and thinking

About him.

I try to shake away flashes of the
Nod he gave me.

He did not look like someone who was
Missing me.

He did not look like he regretted our
Break-up.

He looked like a person
Glorying

At being the centre
Of attention.

"What do you normally do on choir nights?"
Flora asks

And when she does, I realise I'd forgotten
All about it.

Choir is every Thursday evening
And before him

I usually would walk into town
To eat and wait

For it to begin by playing on
My phone

Wandering around shops
Until

I was allowed passage into the
Rehearsal room.

I did not do any of this
After him.

"I walk into town and just
Hang out."

"Well then," Flora says with conviction.
"Let's go."

Bar

a segment of music bounded by vertical lines

Flora talks in | a strange rhythm |
it sounds like she | is always on | the beat.
Flora's hair is | smooth and twisted | into a bun |
as if she is | preparing to | perform.
Flora stands straight | her back upright |
as if she is | about to go | on stage.

Composer

a person who writes music

I want to know so much
About her.

"What do you like?" I ask
Because

I want to say
Something.

I am already cringing at the stupidity
Of the question.

Flora doesn't sneer. She looks
Thoughtful

Like she really wants to consider
Her answer

Or isn't really sure what
She likes.

"What do I like?" she repeats,
Her hands

Loosening the knot
Of her tie,

Unbuttoning the top buttons
On her shirt.

I do the same though I have never
Done this before.

Never tried to give myself
The illusion

Of freedom from
This uniform

Before I strip it off on my eventual
Return home.

"I like composers," she says,
With conviction.

"Composers?" I ask wanting to be sure
I heard her

"Yess" she says. "Yes."
Flora likes composers.

Not just the music, but the composers
Themselves.

She likes to know about their lives.
Likes to know about what drove them.
What made them create.
What broke them.

Flora especially likes
Composers

Who weren't appreciated
When alive.

We walk towards town and Flora tells me
About her favourites.

She doesn't ask anything about
Me.

And I don't ask anything else
About her.

Ensemble

a group of musicians who perform together

I used to love
Choir

It made me happy
To be singing

With people that only
Care about

How high my voice
Can go

And if the notes I sing are
Sharp or flat.

I can feel it pressing
Against me

The same urge
To leave

To forget I ever cared
About singing.

The urge to not contribute
To not take part.

To go home.
To not practise.

I do not want the joy to be sucked
out of this place.

This sanctuary.
This life.

To avoid eye contact with that concerned face,
I let

My focus wander, into the eyes
Of Flora.

She smiles a real smile, and I return
A fake one.

Hoping that, in time,
This can be real.

Ernst

serious

"Did you know," Flora says as
We wait

After choir for our parents
To pick us up,

"Bach had twenty children?" I did not
Know that.

I am astounded that he was able
To compose

The amount of music
He did

While apparently having
A lot of sex

And so many children at home.
"A lot of them died,"

Flora says, her words, as always,
To the point.

"How many?" I ask, and I am not sure
Why it matters.

"Ten, altogether." A silence lingers
Because

I can't think of what to say about that
Kind of loss.

"He probably had nothing to do with them,"
Flora says

Cutting and cruel
And honest.

I think this has nothing to do
With Bach's parenting.

I realise that Flora
Is private

But she is not
Subtle.

We lean against the cold wall now in a
Comfortable silence.

Looking up each time a car approaches.
"Who is picking you up?"

"My mam," she says.
"It's always my mam."

Calmando

becoming calm

It is incredible and impossible to
Believe

That life seems to settle into a normal
Routine.

After all that dread and
Drama.

Days become as predictable as
Ever.

School is about
Learning and revision.

Choir is about
Learning and rehearsal.

Days of class.
Evenings of homework.
Weekends of revision.

I struggle, feeling like I
Am learning

A lot of this for the very
First time.

Slowly the whispers
Move on

To something else and for
A few weeks

It feels like everything might
Be okay.

Singer

a person who sings

Conversations with Flora are
About music.

We talk about her favourite composers
And mine.

We talk about the different places we have been
Because of music.

We talk about competitions and concerts
Dramas and triumphs.

On a walk to rehearsal one day, I ask a question
So obvious

I know I have avoided asking it because
I did not

Want to answer it
Myself.

"Did you ever play
An instrument?"

Flora takes a moment to consider
Her answer.

This is a habit of hers, I have
Noticed.

Flora thinks about what she is going to say
Before she says it.

Flora gives her answers to questions
A lot of thought.

"I played the piano for a bit," she
Confesses

Like this is some
Dirty secret

That she has never revealed
To anyone.

Like she tried something and it
Didn't work out.

And it is something to be
Ashamed of.

"I am more of a singer," Flora says
With finality.

"I played recorder for a bit," I say, aware
She never asked.

Klar

clear, distinct

Every week we hear about
Matches.

We hear about training and points
And goals.

The anticipation is building, thanks to Gareth
And David.

The Curse will soon
Be lifted.

The principal graciously mentions
The entire team

But he always makes sure to say
The real reason.

His greatness, his focus, his talent
His discipline.

My greatness, my focus, my talent
My discipline.

The score is reported like
Headline news.

Every Monday at the assembly
It is mentioned

And awed whispers roll
Around the hall

As excitement builds that
The Curse

Could be broken
At last.

Doloroso

sorrowful, painful

The Thursday before midterm is full of
Clambering excitement

Students and teachers competing in their
Demonstrations

Of who is more desperate
For a break.

Flora and I spend the day passing notes
Back and forth

Looking forward to our choir rehearsal
Tonight

Where we will do a full run-through
Of the Bach Cantata.

"Once you begin to really perform it,
You will understand it,"

Flora reassures me when I confide
That I am struggling with

Certain parts of the piece and
The questions

Asked in our
Revision tests.

It is a new feeling for me to be struggling
With Music.

But there is something about Bach and
His Cantata

That I cannot keep
A hold of.

Elegy

A song of lament

I am struggling with
Bach's Cantata.

"It is all about suffering."
Flora smiles at me

"I am surprised you aren't connecting
With it more."

Flora doesn't often mention
My break-up

Of which she knows little more
Than it happened.

It is the middle of the day. I get a text
From my mother

Telling me that I need
To miss choir.

My brothers are home.
Of course,

The red carpet needs to
Be rolled out

I wanted to go to choir
To sing

And maybe understand what
Bach

Was trying to say in this
Suffering Cantata.

"Home. Now,"
She replies.

I do what I am told because
I always do.

The battered car in the
Driveway.

My brothers have returned.
Everything must halt.

I go up to my room, without
Saying hello to them.

So irritated by
My mother

It didn't occur to me
To wonder

Why, in the middle of the week,
They are home.

Split

a technique where a musical line or melody is divided and plated by multiple musicians or voices

"It's not time to
Tell her."

"Dad, she is not
A fool."
"She has so much going on.
Exams, and Music.

And that little
Prick."

I don't know what bothers me
More –

That they are speaking
About me

That they are speaking
About him

Or that they are speaking badly
About him.

What right do they have
To stand around

And hold council about what
I should

Feel or
Not feel.

I push into the kitchen feeling
Justified

In my fury about their
Family meeting.

"What do you think you are doing?"
I accuse

Them all but mainly
My mother.

The conductor of this small
Quartet.

"You are always talking
About me."

My mother sighs and my father
Looks exhausted.

Fiachra shakes his head but says
Nothing.

Tadgh is always the one
Quicker to anger.
Quicker to take the bait.
Quicker to comment.

"I know it's hard for you
To believe, Daisy.

But not everything that goes on
In this house

Is about you," he spits,
Venom and spite.

"What is it then? The thing that
You are all discussing

That you seem to think is none of my
Business.

But still made me
Skip choir?"

A thousand conversations
Are had

Through silence, the silent
Looks,

A debate clearly raging between the
Adults.

Because the twins are
Adults now.

Fiachra was never able
To keep a secret.

"Daisy," he says,
"Dad is sick."

That is all that comes out.
His voice cracks.

He turns his back to look
At our father

Who has not moved
Since my arrival.

Tadgh delivers the blow.
"He has cancer.

Thyroid."

I look to my mother, her face
Melting

Into tears and with that look
I realise

Our world has been
SP L IT
SP L IT

Spiegando

unfolding

Cancer is a thing you hear about
From friends.

They talk about dead grandparents and
Aunts and uncles.

It is a thing that is to be feared
From a distance

But safely because it happens
To other people.

"Do you want to talk about it?"
My brothers

Are still in the house trying
To act like

They are not as scared or
As affected.

Like they know everything about
What is going on.

They have no idea
What is going on.

They have no idea how this is going
To end.

"No thanks," I say and I retreat
To my room.

I hear them muttering with my mother
Again.

What they are saying isn't worth
Trying to listen to.

I have questions I want
Answered.

Things I want
To ask.

Cerca la nota

look for the note

Alone that night I begin to
Search for answers

Thyroid cancer:

Symptoms

Treatment plans

Diagnosis

Stages

Survival Chances

Signs

Chemotherapy:

Side Effects

Thyroid Cancer

Definition

Sickness

Treatment

After Care

Things that you can learn about cancer from the internet:

Treatment Plans

Cancer names

Chemotherapy side effects

Radiation side effects

Surgery plans

How cancer progresses
How cancer spreads
Survival rates

Passing note

in part-writing, a note moving
stepwise between two harmony notes
but belonging to either chord

How long has this tumour
Been growing?

Was it with my father during
My concerts?

Was it with him at the twins'
Matches?

Did it join us for
Sunday dinners?

How long has it been a part of
My father?

A companion he never
Asked for.

Wherever he went
Whatever he did.

Waiting
Waiting
Waiting
Waiting

To strike.

Danse macabre

the dance of the dead

"You didn't miss much." Flora is speaking
About choir.

"Why was it your mam wanted you
Home?"

Flora calls her mother 'Ma'
And my mother 'Mam'.

"My brothers came home."
"Oh. That's nice,"

Flora says in a way that implies,
As an only child,

She doesn't fully understand the dynamics
That can emerge

When older siblings
Return home.

I don't say anything to confirm
Whether or not

It was nice.

"Since it's the last day before midterm,"
Ms Willis is speaking,

"I thought we could take a break
From Bach.

But I don't want today to be
A complete doss.

I thought we should listen to some of my
Favourite pieces.

And get inspired for all the practice you
Will be doing."

As she turns her back, I catch
Flora's eye

Expecting to see her eyes waiting
For mine

To share a roll at the idea
That

Any of us would want to hear
Her favourite pieces.

But Flora is leaning over, her chin
In her hands

Waiting for what we
Are about to hear.

"This is because it's about to be
Halloween."

When I hear the first clash
Of violins

I know the piece
Straight away.

Over the music Ms Willis is
Excited

In the same way I used to get
Excited

When I heard a piece of music I
Connected with.

"Saint-Saëns composed this
In 1874.

The Danse Macabre is supposed to
Demonstrate to the audience

The idea of the dead called to attention
By Death himself

To come alive and dance
In the graveyard.

Try to think about all the different lines,
The genius of

His instrument choice and his
Use of rhythm."

I can only think
About

Treatment Plans.

Cancer names.

Chemotherapy side effects.

Radiation side effects.

Surgery plans.

How cancer progresses.

How cancer spreads.

Survival rates.

Ms Willis stops talking and turns up
The volume.

I close my eyes and try not to think
About Google searches

I try not to think about
Skeletons

Dancing on gravestones.

Plainte

a mournful piece lamenting a death or some other unhappy occurrence

Back again
After the midterm

I see David
He sees me

I want to stop him to say
"My Dad has cancer."

To have him ask me to tell him
All about it.

We nod and keep moving
As usual.

I see Shannon.
She sees me.

And I want to stop her and tell her
"My Dad has cancer."

The man who used to drive you to
Birthday parties

And sleepovers and made
You toast.

We ignore each other
As usual.

I want to care less about him
And her

And care more about
My father.

I sit beside Flora who takes notes,
Intently,

And stare out
The window.

The Bach-Werke-Verzeichnis (BWV)

a catalogue of compositions by Johann Sebastian Bach

Flora's favourite composer by far
Is Johann Sebastian Bach.

She talks about him like
They're friends.

She knows everything about
His life.

She connects with his music and
His history.

She talks to me about him
As we walk to choir

Where we will spend two hours
Singing Bach

And on our way to
Music class

Where we will spend
An hour

Talking about Bach and
I cannot stand

To think about Bach for too long
But I

Get caught up in the stories she tells
About a man

Who fathered twenty children
Only ten survived.

A man who composed a cantata
Every week.

Who died blind because a charlatan
Stole his sight.

Marcato

marked, stressed

"Bach loved the recorder," Flora says
One day

As we are walking towards choir
Kicking stones.

“Hum,” I say, thinking
About my father

Who is having surgery
Tomorrow.

“Have you ever played any of
His pieces?”

I have played Bach on the recorder
Many times,

But there is only one piece
That I think about.

“Don’t you ever think about Tchaikovsky?”
I ask.

“Did you know that Tchaikovsky spent his life
Writing music

And allowing another person
To critique

And shape and
Rearrange it?”

“Who was the other person?”
“Why does it matter?”

And I don’t know
Why it matters.

In my mind it seems there is
A time when

It might be
Acceptable

To let someone else's opinion
Change you.

Depending on who that
Person was.

"A lot of his original drafts are
Lost now."

Flora views this as
A tragedy.

Could his
First drafts,

The ones he composed for
Himself,

The ones he composed
Alone,

The ones that are now lost,
Have been better?

Duramente
harshly

"Have you given any
Thought

To your practical
Yet?"

I ask Flora while we are
Walking

To find
Somewhere

We can eat chips and
Drink Coke

And get some energy before we go
To choir.

I want to know what she is going
To do

Because I still
Have no idea

What I am going
To do.

"Not really," Flora says
Her answer stiff

And I question, not for
The first time,

What it is about music that makes
Flora seem relaxed

And on edge at the
Same time.

Morendo

dying away

"What about you?" she asks and to give
An answer

I name six pieces of music
That I could sing

From musicals that could be accompanied
By a piano.

"You are only thinking about singing?"
She asks.

There are many things that
Exist between us.

The version of me that existed
Before I knew her.

The version of her that existed
Before she knew me.

There are many things
I am hiding

From her.
From my parents.
From myself.

Flora is waiting for me to say
Something.

Fuoco

with fire, wild and fast

"My dad has cancer." This is
The first time

I have said the words
Aloud.

I don't know what I expected
From Flora.

Sympathetic words.
Shock.

Tears are building and I cannot
Stop them

From pouring down
My cheeks.

I don't want Flora to
See me

As a person
Who cries.

I do not want her to
Think there

Is always
Something

Going on
With me.

I pull the sleeve of my
Uniform jumper

Down over my hand
And do my best

To wipe the tears and snot
From my face

Leaving a variety of
Trails

That will remain there for
At least a week –

My mother will
Only wash

My uniform jumper every other
Friday.

"You seem really upset," she says.
"You must like your da.

I wonder what that's like.
To have a da you'd be sorry
To have die."

I am rage and sickness
And pure fury

"What the fuck is wrong with you?"
I hiss into her face

"He's not going to die."
I no longer care

What this girl thinks
About me.

"He might."
She said that.

She.
Said.
That.

"Never. Say that. Again."

I leave her standing on her own, her face
Unreadable.

Molto

much, very

Facts about composers I know thanks to Flora

Beethoven didn't like to shower.
Mozart might have been poisoned and they don't know where his body is.
Chopin's body was buried in Paris, but his heart was buried in Poland.
Debussy loved the ladies, and the ladies loved him.
Tchaikovsky loved mushrooms.
Bach had twenty children but only half survived.
Bach once hit a bassoonist and spent a month in jail for it.
Bach would fight his students.
Bach loved coffee.

Facts about Flora I know thanks to Flora

Flora sings alto.
Flora hates her father.

Pianissimo

very softly

If my mother notices that I have
Come home

Straight after school and not
Gone to choir

If my mother notices that my eyes are red
And my face is blotchy

If my mother notices that I did no
Homework that night

That I sat in the living room staring
At the television

Flicking from channel to channel
Settling on nothing

If my mother notices
That I went to bed

At eight p.m.

Without saying goodnight
Without having a shower
Without getting a glass of water
Without playing with the cat
Without laying out my uniform
Without preparing my lunch
Without packing my bag for school

She does not say anything.

The next morning when
I wake up

My parents are
Both gone.

Today my father
Is having surgery.

Before they left for
The hospital

I didn't say anything.

S.A.T.B.

describes a score for a choir in four parts:
Soprano, Alto, Tenor, Bass

My family like to think that
We are in tune

S - Me
A - Tadgh
T - Fiachra
B - Dad

A perfect Quartet guided by my mother
The conductor

Keeping time and bringing order
To chaos.

Each of us expected to know
Our own line.

The rest of them never   a beat
                                        miss

I am part of the ensemble but
Unable to match them.

Forte to their pianissimo.
Loud when they are quiet.
Quiet when they are loud.

Lately, I have missed my cues
No matter how hard

I try to keep up
No matter how prepared

Or well-rehearsed I feel I keep
Missing my cues.

Sometimes, just sometimes,
It feels like

The conductor has forgotten to tell me
When to enter.

Leid

grief, pain

The house is empty.
Silent

I cannot stand the sound
Of nothing

Sitting there waiting
For news

Wondering when the time
Will come

That the blade will cut into
My father's skin

And peel back the flesh
To reveal

Just what it is that lurks
within him.

I can't bear the

silence.

Perdendosi

losing itself, dying away

I ask Alexa to fill the house
With music.

Jumping from genre
To genre.

And there is no reason to
My requests

Because there doesn't
Have to be.

I think about calling
Flora

To talk about yesterday
But

I don't want to be the one who
Is always chasing

Someone else
Anymore.

I do not want to
Think or talk

About the true things
She said.

That he might die.

I just need the music to pound
In my ears

To reach down
Inside me

I just want to close my eyes
And fill my soul

With music.

Ermattend

tiring, weakening

It's ten a.m. the next day when
I wake

To a text from
My mother

That's enough.
Go to school.

She hasn't said anything else
About him

Since a quick phone call right after
The surgery.

How is he?
What are they doing?
Is he asleep or awake?
Can he talk?
When will he be home?
When will she be home?

Tomorrow.

I reply waiting for
The resistance.

Waiting for: you have to go today.
Waiting for: we care about your results.
Waiting for: we care about your future.
Waiting for: we care about what happens to you.

The phone vibrates.

Grand.

I want to know when
She is coming home.

I want to know when
He is coming home.

I want to say
There is no food here

I want to tell her
What Flora said.

I want to ask her to
Come home

And take care
Of me.

Loin
distant

Knock.
Knock.

I am on the couch wrapped in a duvet
Cocoon

Flicking without settling on
Anything.

Ignoring the fact that someone
Is at the door.

A person who is here
To give my mother

Thoughts and prayers
Or a mass card.

I settle back into my
Layer

Of comfort but
Now there is

A hammer at the window
A familiar face

Pressing against
The glass

Of the living room
Smiling in.

Flora has come
To my home.

I consider not letting
Her in

But the look on her face
Informs me

That is not
An option.

She has skipped lessons
And found out where I live

Without so much as a
Phone call.

"Well," she says as I pull open
The door

And she pushes past me
Not waiting to learn

Whether or not I welcome
Her visit.

Duodrama

a melodrama for two speakers

Flora is in my home
Surrounded

By photos of my life
Before

I became self-conscious
About things

Like smiling for photos
With my family.

Photos of me
Playing the recorder

At various different
Ages.

Her eyes linger over
Them all

Before she turns and looks
At me.

"You sick?" she asks before
Laughing

At some unknown joke to
Herself

Pulling up when I do not return
A smile.

What has happened to you? I want
To ask her.

What has happened to make you wish
For things

That I fear
In the night?

To make you hope for a fear
I find so shameful

I can only share it with
Internet searches

When everyone else is gone
To sleep.

"You have a guest,"
Flora says,

"You should show me
Around."

I have no idea when my mother
Is coming home

She hasn't called
Or texted

Since her futile attempt to make me
Go to school.

I don't know how she
Could react

If Flora is here when she
Comes home.

But I don't care
What she is feeling.

In relievo

in relief, i.e. a direction to make a melody stand out

I know what is going
To happen

The way I know
Rhythm.

The way I know how to
Find a note.

When she enters
My room

She will not notice the
Mess

I have been
Living in.

Her eyes will have
Been drawn

To that leather case
Exactly where

It has been since my father
Gave it to me.

I want her to go
Home.

I don't have the energy to talk about
Composers

Or have her avoid all the questions
I ask her.

She has reached over and picked up
The case.

My recorder.
The gift from my father.

Who is sick.
Who might die.

"When did you get this?" she asks,
Looking at

The case opened once, never again
Touched.

"My birthday."

I want to snatch it from
Her hands

And demand she
Leaves.

"That was ages ago," she says,
Unclipping the case.

There's a tightness
In my chest

A useless protectiveness as her fingers
Grasp the black wood

Pulling its three pieces from
Its leather carrying case.

I am not the first person
To take it from the case.

That honour has now gone
To Flora.

"Daisy," Flora asks,

"What happened?
Tell me what happened."

Gebunden

bound

I have no idea how to say
How ashamed

I feel and how lost I am without
Music.

I start with the easiest
Part.

"He broke up with me." She nods.
This part she knows.

"Three weeks after we had sex
For the first time.

He broke up with me. After all I did
To help him

With his training and his
Mindset and his

Hurling and then I said
I was ready

And he never said he didn't
Love me."

"When?" Flora asks. "When
Did this happen?"

"The night before my Grade Eight
Exam."

Flora deflates, satisfied
And disappointed.

"And what happened?"
"I couldn't play."

"You made mistakes?"
"No. I just stood there.

In silence. I didn't start.
I didn't try."

"Because he broke up
With you?"

Flora can see the truth
That I have

Been trying to deny to even
Myself –

It's easier
To blame him.

"I didn't know it
My mind went blank

The music made no sense
I didn't practise."

"Do you know why you haven't
Played since?"

"No," I say, because
I don't know.

"It's because you are
Punishing yourself.

The only way you know
How."

Gradatamente

gradually

"You need to play this."
It's simple

The way she says it.
"You can play it."

"Ms Willis wants me to play
Grade Five pieces."

Flora sighs and nods and
Understands

That I am not as good
As I used to be.

That I am not as practised
As I used to be.

That I used to be better.
That I should be better.

And that my Music teacher
Has noticed.

"It's embarrassing,"
I confess.

Flora won't say there is nothing to be
Embarrassed about.

That is not the kind of person
Flora is.

She speaks the truth
As she sees it.

"It is. It's embarrassing.
But you aren't

The first girl to lose her mind over
A boy

You aren't the first person
To give up

Their life because they fell
In love

With someone they
Shouldn't have.

You need to stop acting like you are.
You need to stop acting like you're special.

What happened is not what made
You special.

Your music is what made
You special

And it can make you
Special again."

"I don't think that I can,"
I whisper.

"Your da deserves to hear you
Play this for him."

Tears, so easily summoned,
Are here again.

"I don't know where
to start."

"Yes, you do," Flora says,
"You need to go back

To the beginning. We are going to start
Right now."

Flora hands me three pieces and
With shaking hands

I begin to put them
Together.

Scale

a sequence of notes ascending or descending stepwise

It is
Time
Daisy
To figure out
Who you are
Who you
Want to be
Where
You want
To go
And if
Music can
Take you
There

Lento

slow

"What do you want to play?" A few hours
Later

Flora is still here listening to me
Do scales

Up and down, her eyes
Focused on me.

What she is
Really asking:

What do you want to be?
How hard do you want to work?
Do you think you can be as good
As you used to be?
Do you want to be as good as you used to be?

I think about my father
And my mother

Learning the true meaning of
In sickness and in health.

I think about what I
Know about

Chemotherapy and radiation
And surgeries.

About the things they have
Told me

And the things
They haven't

And what the internet tells me
About

Survival rates and
Side effects.

I think about David and
The time

I spent with him that wasn't
Time practising

And the time wasted since
Our break-up.

And about Ms Willis, who thinks
I have lost

Three grades worth of talent and ability
And hard work.

"The Allemande from Partita
1013."

Flora raises an eyebrow. "Bach?
That's a difficult piece.

Have you ever played it before?"
I say nothing.

Because I have played it
Before.

I have practised and
Played it.

I have tried to play it.
And failed to play it.

On the day when I lost
My mind

And forgot who I was
When I

Let myself get so caught up
In his world

I forgot to live in
My own.

Flora has the answer.
Of course, she does.

"You fucked it up.
In the exam.

That is the piece
You fucked up. Bach."

Her favourite composer.
Flora now understands

Why I never cared that much
About the Cantata.

Why Bach is the one
I always avoid.

Why her facts about him are the most
Uninteresting.

It hangs between us, this truth
That I ruined

Flora's favourite composer
For myself.

"Then," Flora says, "you need
To practise."

Da capo

from the beginning

"How much practice?"
Flora frowns

And pulls out her
Phone.

"How long do you think
You lost

Because of him? Be honest.
Really honest."

That disgusted feeling
I get

Is here but this is
Flora

And I need to know
What she

Thinks and how much
It will take.

"Five months."
"Five months.

Let's assume you would have
Done

Two to two and a half hours
A day.

And we have eight weeks to
The practical."

Her fingers dance on
Her phone

Screen and I notice
How carefully

And delicately they
Move as

They do the math to
Deliver my fate.

Of what it may take
To be

What I was
Before.

"Five hours
A day."

Five hours
A day.

Idée fixe

obsession

How do most people play the recorder?

It comes in three pieces.
They pick it up

And they put those pieces
Together.

They make sure those pieces are lined
The right way.

They make sure
They can cover all the holes

With their fingers
Comfortably.

They keep a steady flow of air –
It's essential

They know that they need to
Control

Their lungs
Their breath.
They keep steady.
They keep straight.
They keep going.

How do I play the recorder?

I spend time thinking about how good I
Used to be.

I spend time thinking about all the time
I wasted.

I spend time thinking
About the money

My recorder playing cost
My parents

And how it is a waste for them now that
I am a person

Who used to play
The recorder

Now that I am the girl who used to be known
For playing the recorder

Now that I am a girl who has in her hand
A brand-new recorder

That she is yet
To play.

Exercise

a passage specifically designed for the
practice of vocal or instrumental techniques
and with no aesthetic intent

We go to school and do
Our best

To focus on the subjects
We cannot ignore

During the day before
Retreating

To the small music rooms designed
For practice.

Flora issues
Instructions

I do my best to not think about
All the time I spent

In this room
With him.

Flora is a hard
Taskmaster.

She refuses to accept
My excuses.

I play the pieces she gives me
Over and over

Until it's time
To go home.

Flora has looked at videos
Of me playing

Listened to recordings that
My parents continued

To make long after my talent ceased to be
A novelty.

Something flashes in her eyes
As I play.

I am nothing like I used to be
My instinct is gone.

Flora never says it out loud, but I know
She is thinking,

"How could you have let this
Happen?"

Plainte
complaint

I dig around in my music bag
And pull out a score

Well-marked with thumbed pages
And folded corners.

"Let's see what you have then,"
Flora says

As I bend back
The cover.

As I turn the pages of the score
I can see notes in my own handwriting

'No breath.'
'Pull back.'
'Less here.'

I can see myself in
Those rehearsals

A creature that worked
On habit.

If you are given
An instruction

You make a note of it
In your score.

Even if you are on your phone
Obsessively checking

For a text that was promised
That had not arrived.

Even as you are clicking and
Scrolling

Knowing there is
Nothing there

Because you have not gotten
A notification.

Even if you are consumed by someone
Else's world.

If you are given an instruction
You make a note

And hope that your future self can
Figure out

What the note means
Or what it refers to.

I look at these notes
To myself.

Another part of my life I no longer
Recognise.

Partita

originally the name for a single-instrumental piece of music. J.S. Bach sometimes used it for collections of musical pieces

From this point my life is
About

Two works by J.S. Bach.
One, the Cantata 78,

Composed to be performed
As a group.

This will be sung with
My choir.

Supported.

Mistakes can be hidden
When you

Sing as a group.

I will study this
Work

Alongside every Music student
in the country.

Alongside my class.
Alongside Flora.

Two,

The one

I must perform **alone.**

Allemande from Partita 1013.
A solo piece.

Written for a flute.
Playable on a recorder.

A silent room
No audience

No shuffling
No fidgeting.

No fiddling
With programmes.

A room filled with
Nothing.

Standing in front of
An examiner

Whose only job is to
Look at me

And watch for
Mistakes.

Pietoso

pitifully, tenderly

"Bach didn't write this piece for
The recorder."

"I know."

"He wrote it for the flute."

"I know."

"Traverso flute."

"I know. I know. I know.

Why are you talking to me
Like I

Don't know that?
Don't know anything?"

Flora looks at me
Calm as always.

"Because you aren't
Acting

Like you know anything
About it."

How can it be that I cannot
Hold my breath

In the way that
I used to.

That my fingers cannot move as quickly
Or as lightly.

"Could that be possible?" I practically spit
At Flora

In a burst of frustration after stumbling
To the end of the piece.

Embarrassed that she has
Witnessed it.

"Is it possible that it is all
Gone?"

Flora tilts her head cocked to one side
Her face contemplative.

"No. I don't think that it's possible
It's gone.

I do think it is possible that you have lost
Your confidence.

I do think it's possible that you have lost
Your faith in yourself.

I do think it's possible that you have lost
Your fire.

I do think it's possible that your hands
Are rusty.

I do think it's possible your lungs
Are weaker.

I do think it's possible that you have lost
Your way.

I do think it's possible that you can find
Your way back.

But I think that it's time that you
Stop complaining.

I think it's time you stop letting David
Control your life.

I think it's time you
Get over yourself

And start to practise like you have
Lost it all.

And you want it
Back."

Sforzando

sudden stress on a note or chord

What should a player expect when they are practising recorder five hours a day?

According to the internet:

1. Physical fatigue - you will feel exhausted.
2. Back pain - holding your posture can cause pain in the neck and shoulders.
3. Mental fatigue - you won't always be able to focus.
4. Burnout - a decrease of enjoyment in the task.
5. Isolation - you won't see anyone because you are practising.

What should a patient expect when they are getting treatment for thyroid cancer?

According to the internet:

1. Physical fatigue - you will feel exhausted.
2. Back pain, neck pain, arm pain, leg pain, pain.
3. Mental fatigue - you won't be able to think.
4. Burnout - a decrease of enjoyment in everything.
5. Isolation - risk of infection; you won't see anyone because they might kill you.

Presto

quick

"Here are some things I think you
Should know

About the Bach Cantata
That are interesting."

Flora is again talking about
Her favourite subject.

"For the Leaving?" I ask, desperate
For any help

That this might give in me passing
My Music exam.

"Well," Flora says. "Some of it might
Be useful, sure.

The rest of it is just
Interesting.

It might not help you
In exams

But it will help you
Understand it more

So you can sing it
Better."

I don't really care about
Singing it

Better but I keep that
To myself.

I let Flora ramble on about
The things

She thinks I need to know about
Bach and his Cantata

None of which will help me for my
Leaving Cert paper.
We round the corner to our lockers
And I see it.

Ricochet

rebound

"Daisy?" Flora's voice
Is speaking.

She turns her head to look
Behind her

Her eyes landing where
Mine are locked

And though she is seeing
What I am seeing

She is not grasping it as quickly
As I am.

"What are we looking at?" she says
Because Flora

Does not know the back of his head
Like I do.

Flora does not know the shape of her hands
Like I do.

"Daisy," Flora speaks again,
"What's wrong?"

How could she not see
What is happening

The blatantness of how they are
Intertwined

Right in the hall, students milling
About.

Some, like me, are stopping
To gape

While the rest are walking past
Not interested.

How could anyone not care
About this.

Right in this place where I used
To kiss him

David and Shannon have found
Their way

To each other

Éteint

extinguished, barely audible

Shannon never understood why
My weekends

Were dominated by practice
And performance

And music.

Shannon is the kind of girl
Who likes

The kind of things her
Friends like.

We had the same things.

The same school, the same
Playgrounds.

Her parents, friends with
My parents.

Her brother, friends with
My brothers.

Shannon is not a girl who has things
Of her own.

She borrows hobbies, interests, clothes
And personalities.

Her life has been dictated by
Others.

At first, she tried to follow me
To music.

I see her differently
Now.

That may not be fair to her
Or me.

But it seems when she could not
Keep up and

Saw that I was more talented
More admired

She found ways to pull
Me down.

Schmerzlich

painfully

In my head I am walking over and
Demanding

What the fuck
Is going on.

In my head,
I am screaming

In my head
I am strong
And forceful
And indignant
And righteous

In real life I am
None of those things

I am just a broken-hearted
Girl

Watching her ex-boyfriend
Kiss her ex-best friend.

Say nothing
Do nothing.
Keep going.

I turn and head out
The front door

Past a puzzled
Flora

And baffled
Ms Willis

And indignant
Principal.

I hear his voice calling
After me

"Where do you think
You are going?"

I need to get home

Where everything can be
Understood.

It's raining and I have
No jacket.

The house is locked, and I have
No keys.

It's Friday and I have
No bag.

I need to go home
To my mother.

To her soothing voice.
Her caring eyes.

Her knowing words.
Her comfort meals.

Her cups of tea.
Her hot-water bottles.

Stark

strong, loud

I burst through the front
Door

Into the face of
My mother.

"What are you doing here?"

Her voice is sharp.
Cold.

A bow screeching down a violin
With abandon.

She was
Expecting me.

I can hear
My father.

Coughing. Retching.

Smell the faint fumes
Of vomit.

A bad day from the poison pumped
Into his body.

Reacting to its dual purpose of saving
And weakening him.

"The school called."

I see my reflection in the mirror
Behind her.

It is obvious that I have been running
And crying

Eyes black from mascara and
Eyeliner

Spots peeking through
Streaked foundation.

If I can see it, she can
See it.

"I just needed to come home."
My voice is tiny

In a world where everything is
Audible.

"To not be around
David."

"Daisy, I cannot believe you are still
Going on about this.

Do you think I have time
To deal

With calls from
Your school?

You need to deal with
Your life.

I gave you the choice.
You chose to stay.

Do you understand that your father
Might die?

And all you can do is act like a brat
Over some boy.

Not everything is about you,
Daisy.

Go Back.
To School."

She is not
My mother.

She is a wife whose husband
Is sick.

And a daughter
Failing him.

I don't have any comeback to her
Accusations.

I know they are true
Because

They are the same things I say
To myself.

I turn my back.
On her pain.
On her fury.

And, in just a few moments
From now,

Her regret.

My mother is not cruel.

She is exhausted.
She is stressed.
She is terrified.
I don't care.

She is still
My mother.

She only sees what they are
Going through.

And I only see what I am
Going through.

I am sick.

Sick of being
The reliable child.

"I am not going back
To school."

We stare at each other
And I think

She is going
To slap me.

She's moving, grabbing
Her keys.

"Fine. I don't care what you do,"
She says.

"You've made that very obvious,"
I snap to her back.

The front door slams and leaves me
Standing in the hall

Listening to the sound
Of my father retching.

Estinto

extinguished, i.e. barely audible

I want to be able to talk to
Him

About all the things
That are happening.

About the times when things
Were easier.

When it was just us
Driving around.

To tell him I am practising
Again

That I am playing my new
Recorder.

He is lying on the couch.
Sick and tired.

Asleep in front of the
Television.

I do my best to move towards
The flickering box

To turn it off and leave him
In peace

"Daisy," he whispers
As I move

To leave the room.
"I'm sorry," I say

Turning to look at his
Pale skin

His thin face and his body
Wasting away.

"I didn't mean to wake
You up."

"Sit," he says,
"Talk to me.

I want to hear about
School."

I sit in the chair beside him
Stomach churning.

I don't have anything to tell him
About school.

I have been doing nothing and he
Knows that.

Because he is
My father.

And he knows me better
Than anyone.

It feels like I can
Talk to him about

All the things that have
Happened

All the ways I have wronged him
Or been wronged

And finally ease the weight that has been
On my shoulders.

Before I get a chance to figure out where
To begin

He has fallen
Back asleep.

And I sit with him until
The sun sets.

Cracked note

used when a musician, particularly a vocalist or a wind instrument player, produces a note with poor tonal accuracy, causing it to sound off-key or out of tune

I am sneaking my way out of the
Living room

When my mother appears back
From her temper walk

I brace myself for her disappointment
In me.

"Daisy." It's as far as she gets
Before the cracks

Begin to show in her voice and
On her face.

I say nothing and she
Tries again.

"Daisy," she says and stops and tries
Again.

"Daisy," and on this third time, she has
Found her voice.

"I know this is hard
For you.

You deserve to be allowed to rebel
And be able

To be heartbroken and have space
To make mistakes.

But I need you to look after yourself
For a while.

Your brothers will look after each other,
I will look after your father.

I want you to know
That I know

How unfair this is.
How cruel this is.

What I am asking
From you.

I am sorry to ask this
Of you.

I need you to grow up, love."

Intermezzo

in the middle, a piece of music inserted between two parts of a performance

I used to talk to David on the phone
Until the sun rose.

I used to talk to Shannon on the phone
Until the sun rose.

I used to practise music
Until the sun rose.

Now I stare at the ceiling
Until the sun rises.

Now I worry about my family
Until the sun rises.

Now I think about what David is doing
Until the sun rises.

Now I wonder what people are saying
Until the sun rises.

Opera

a dramatic work in one or more acts, set to music for singers and instrumentalists

Christmas exams are over
Relaxation can begin.

There is a buzz in the air that feels
Like more than

The usual excitement of the impending
Break.

Flora appears at my side
Her eyes

Beaming with the kind of
Excitement

That can only come
From gossip.

"Something has happened,"
She says.

That I was detained with Ms Willis at the
Precise moment

Shannon and David chose to have
A blazing fight in

The school corridor could be luck
Or fate but

Thanks to Flora's detailed
Retelling

I might as well have
Been there.

The accusations Shannon has
Thrown in

His direction fall to my ear as
Deeply familiar.

From the mundane and predictable
To the utterly offensive.

Flora deems the row to be impressive
And theatrical.

Nothing her fault
Everything his.

Flora says it was by far the
Most exciting

Thing that has happened since
She arrived here.

Carol

a song, often one associated with Christmas
or Easter, but doesn't have to be seasonal

Christmas break is a relief of
Cold nights and

Lazy days that could almost
Feel normal.

My brothers sleeping till
Noon.

Calling to each other through
The house

Begging me to bring them
Glasses of water.

My mother making toast
And coffee

Doing her best to host
Her family.

My father doing his best
To stay alert

And make this Christmas
Like the others.

If he sits down, he falls
Asleep

Only to awake with
A jolt later

Annoyed with us all for
Letting him

Miss out on
Any fun.

Annoyed that we dared to let him
Rest.

The letter addressed to my
Parents

With the school's crest
On the corner

Arrives when my mother and brothers
Are out

And my father is asleep in front of
The fire.

I take it knowing that no one
Will notice.

I tear open the envelope and scan the letters
Reflecting on

The evidence of the lack of interest
And work

I am doing in this final
All-important year.

A list of Cs is not what is expected
Of me.
I have done slightly better
In Music with a B

But there was no practical, so this is no
Indication

Of what my result will actually
Look like.

Replica

repeat, reprise

January is:
Bach and treatment
Bach and infection
Bach and worry
Bach and stress
Bach and sleep
Bach and Flora
Bach and study
Bach and classes
Bach and revision
Bach and nothing
Bach and everything
Bach and Bach

Forza

force

February brings a welcome midterm
But there is

An atmosphere the moment I
Come back

To those corridors that are
So cold

With no heating
And no souls

To wander down it
For the last week.

I find Flora at the
Lockers

Watching the movement around her
With interest.

"Something has happened."
There is a buzz,

A tittering of news being passed
From ear to ear

Student to student.
Teacher to teacher.

Flora gets it first and passes the news:
"David's gone."

David's gone?
David's gone.

It doesn't take long for a version
Of the real story

To make its way through
The entire year.

The fight witnessed was
Not the first such

Incident and David's
Mother,

Concerned that girls were distracting
Him

From his Leaving Cert studies, sent
Him to the grind school.

Taking with him
Any chance

Our school had of breaking
The Curse.

Polyphonic

producing or involving many sounds or voices

Whatdoyouknow? Nothing. Whatdoyouknow?
Theteachersarefurious. Theprincipaliswalking
aroundwithafacelikethunder.
Whendidithappen? OverChristmas?
Theyneversaidanything. TheytoldtheschoolonFriday.
Friday? Theymusthaveknown. Whatdoesitmean?
He'sgone. He'sgone. He'sgone. He'sgone.
He'sgone. He'sgone. He'sgone. He'sgone.
He'sgone. He'sgone. He'sgone. He'sgone.
Toagrindschool.
Agrindschool. Agrindschool. Agrindschool.
Agrindschool. Agrindschool. Agrindschool.
Hismotherisfurious. Hismotherisfurious.
Hismotherisfurious.
She'sbeencryingallweekend. Whichone? Daisy?
Notheotherone.
Whosefaultisit? Hisparentsdidn'tlikethedrama.

Thedrama? Thedrama thedrama thedrama.
Andwhocausesthedrama?
Thosefuckingbitches.
Andnowwe'llneverwinthecup.
Thebitches. Thebitches. Thebitches.

Because of them? Because of them.

Diminuendo

becoming less loud

Do you ever wish you could get smaller and smaller until the time finally comes when you can just disappear?

Einsatz

entrance, cue

Flora is trying to reassure me
That no one rational

Would blame me for
David leaving.

Both of us aware that
Teenagers

Are not known
To be rational.

We are coming up towards our
Maths room when

I see the back of a familiar blond
Head.

Shannon turns and is barrelling
Towards me

Ferocity on her face
Tears in her eyes

"You are so
Pathetic.

You couldn't just accept that he
Moved on.

I am so sick of watching you
Mope around.

We had to see that every day and he
Felt sorry

For you but I didn't.
I know you.

This is your fault!" she screams,
Reaching mania.

"They made him leave
Because of you."

Shannon is the kind of girl
Who blames

Other people for things that happen
To her.

Shannon is the kind of girl who could
Not believe

He would leave her
Unless it has

Something to do
With me.

It couldn't have been that he wanted
To go.

That he didn't care about
This school,

About her and that
Stupid curse.

I realise too late
That Shannon

Is pulling back
A fully

Closed fist and aiming
For my face.

The idea is too
Strange.

Too bizarre to be
Real.

This girl who used to be
My friend.

That girl who used to know
My secrets.

This girl who told me all
Her secrets.

Before I can move.
Before I can breathe.

A hand appears out of the corner of my eye
Reaching

Moving faster than my brain can
Move.

Quicker than I can
Take in.

Shannon is screaming, her hand
Gripped

To the side of her
Head.

And Flora stands,
Her face unchanged

Looking down at
Her trophy.

A handful of blond hair
Extension.

The victor amongst the resulting
Chaos.

Suspensions

accented non-chord tones occurring on downbeats

All of us are suspended and
Informed

We are very lucky it wasn't
Expulsion.

Protests from Flora that
I had nothing

To do with her decision to
Rip out

Shannon's hair fell on
Deaf ears.

We are separated into different
Corridors

To await our parents who would bring
The real consequences.

Shannon's mother arrived
First

Shrieking about assault and
Court cases.

Looking for someone to
Blame.

The principal shushed her with
A gentle reminder

Of the time he convinced another family
To ignore that

Shannon knocked out their daughter's
Two front teeth

With a hockey stick when we were in
Third Year.

The next parent to arrive
was Flora's dad.

Though I had never seen him
I knew him.

His face looked like
The stone

From which hers
Was carved.

I don't know what I was expecting of
This man

Of whom Flora had nothing
Kind to say.

I was not expecting a man who looked
Open and fatigued.

A man who did not show any anger
Towards her.

A man who did not express
Any disappointment.

A man who tried to put his arm
Around his daughter

And was shown nothing but
Resentment

As she shook off this gesture of comfort
And protection.

I was so mesmerised by the strange coupling
As they

Made their way towards the car
I didn't notice

A familiar form moving slowly
In my direction.

It is not my mother
It is my father
My poor father.

Weak.
Tired.
Thin.
Sick.

Dragged to school from his
Sick bed.

To account for his wayward
Daughter

Who does nothing to help him
And her mother.

And is now getting into fights
In school.

I cannot look at him as we
Walk to our car.

"Your mother has gone to get
Her hair done.

I didn't want to bother her.
We can

Talk about it when
She gets home."

Doppio

double the speed

It is sitting in the drive when we
Pull up.

That familiar battered
Ford Fiesta.

"Your brothers got home
This morning.

Your mother will be cooking
A big dinner."

Those bastards.

Of course they are home
For this.

My father goes straight for the
Living room

Sinking his drained body
Into his chair.

"I'll make you tea,
Daddy."

That old name for him slipping out
Naturally.

"Thanks, love," he says
Weak voiced.

In the kitchen, I feel them
Behind me.

Entering the room like
Two judges

Arrived just in time to deliver
Their sentence.

"I'll make the tea,
Daddy."

One of the voices behind me
Is cruelly mimicking.

Turning, I take in their dishevelled
Appearance.

Out last night and no doubt they have
Brought home

Plenty of laundry for my mother
To do.

"We can't believe you," Tadgh says.

"Fighting at school," Fiachra says.

"Could you not cop on," Tadgh says.

"Dad is sick," Fiachra says.

"In case you hadn't noticed," Tadgh says.

"You can't get it together for him," Fiachra says.

"To give Mam a bit of help," Tadgh says.

"You need to grow up, Daisy," Fiachra says.

My mother's words, said without a fraction
Of the care.

Fortissimo
very loud

Rage, so close always,
Is here again.

Bring a new feeling.
Relief.

Relief that it can finally find
Two targets

To whom I can say
Anything

And they still have
To love me.

"Fuck off.
Both of you."

The kettle is boiling as I stride
Towards them.

They try to step back but meet
The kitchen wall.

I can smell evidence of
The night before.

Beer and cigarettes. I take in
Their crumpled clothes.

"You aren't here. You have no
Idea

What it is like for him, for her,
For me.

Every.
Day.

I can't hug him
Anymore.

Constantly worried he will get
An infection.

There is always something
New.

A new treatment, a new medication,
A new side effect.

The smell of those supplements he needs
To drink.

And the sound of the retching and
Mam crying.

Every day.
She cries."

"We didn't know that,"
Tadgh says

Defensive as always.
Fiachra nods.

"Of course you didn't fucking
Know that.

You are not here.
And when

You do bother to turn up
You have

Mam running around after you,
Cooking dinners,

Washing and ironing for
You.

Dad says you got here
This morning.

So why didn't one of you come
And pick me up

Instead of making him drive when
He is wrecked?"

I turn my back on them to
Make the tea.

They are still there as I
Pour milk

And put biscuits on
A plate.

Silenced.
Stunned.

"Can you move?"
I ask.

They separate, one
Going left

The other
Going right.

In the sitting room, my father
Is watching

Keeping Up with the
Kardashians.

The remote on the armchair
By his side.

"Do you want me to change it,
Daddy?"

I ask, as I put the tea down
Next to him.

"Would you mind, love?
This shite."

"Tell me when to stop," I say
Flicking to channels

For my father.
My champion.

Who was so exhausted
From his treatments

He couldn't muster
The energy

To change the channel
To something

He would enjoy
Watching.

Neither of my brothers come
Into the room.

And my father and I sit
Together.

His untouched tea slowly
Going cold.

Herzlich

heartfelt, affectionate

I don't want to sit at home
And wait

For my mother to return to
Deliver

The necessary admonishments of
My behaviour.

My father is asleep and my brothers
Are sulking.

I slip up to my bedroom and grab
My recorder.

I need to apologise to Flora and
Thank her

For being that kind of
Friend.

I want to go and see her to tell her
I am sorry

That she is suspended
Because of me.

I want to thank her for
Her friendship.

I want to show her how much
I have practised.

Though I have never
Been invited

To her home I know exactly
Where Flora lives

Because in small towns everyone
Knows

What houses are being bought
And sold.

There is no car
In the driveway

But I know this is the right house
Because

Through the window I can see posters,
On the wall

Of an upstairs bedroom, of Bach
And Mozart and Beethoven.

I step forward, ring the bell
And wait.

The man who collected Flora
From school

Who tried to embrace her and was
Shaken off

Answers the door and smiles at the sight
Of me.

"Daisy," he says though he has never
Met me.

It fills me with warmth to think
About Flora

Talking about me at home
With her family.

He waits for me to speak as it takes
A moment

For me to remember why
I am here.

"I wanted to apologise
To Flora."

Flora's father sighs and steps
Backwards

Gesturing that I should step
Over the threshold.

He leads me into a warm open-plan
Kitchen

That doesn't look quite like
It houses

A fully unpacked and settled
Family.

"You don't have anything to
Apologise for,"

Flora's dad says, leaning against
The kitchen counter

And picking up a cup of tea he'd
Clearly been enjoying

In peace before I
Arrived here.

"No one here blames you
For Flora.

Everyone in this house is very
Aware that

Flora makes up her
Own mind."

I hope I do not look as awkward
As I feel

Standing in the kitchen
With Flora's dad

Who is speaking about her
With an edge

In his tone and my mind
Is wandering

To the few things that Flora has told me
About him

None of them positive.
None of them kind.

Modulation

the process of changing from one key to another within a composition

"Is that your new recorder?" He points to my hand which grips the handle of its leather case.

"Can I see it?"

I hand it over and watch his expert hands flick open the box and put the pieces together, twisting at just the right place. Something doesn't feel right about this.

"Do you mind?" he asks, but before I can answer, he has pursed his lips and is playing my recorder.

"It's a nice sound." He nods, approving, oblivious to this violation. He drops it from his mouth but does not give it back.

"Flora doesn't play anymore," he says.

"She was one of the greatest pianists I have ever seen. It was like she came out ready to change the shape of the world through music. She would compose in her sleep. I know it's hard to imagine. When I would check on her at night, I would see her fingers moving in the air. She would wake up and write music as she poured her cornflakes. Chocolate milk. I shouldn't have let her. But I could never say no, to Flora." He sighs and sips from his cup, still with my recorder in his other hand.

"She doesn't play anymore, because of me. I am trying to change that. I am trying to make it up to her." He looks at me and I see the face of so many dads I have known in my life. The ones waiting at the school gates, sitting in their cars outside music lessons, listening to the radio, waiting for their children to come out.

I am trying to keep up with what he is saying but also thinking he must be mad. Flora doesn't play music. Flora does not play an instrument. Flora sings. We have spent days and nights talking about music and how it is in our lives, and she has encouraged me to not let my gift slip away.

"I don't understand" is all I can think to say, because it is true. I don't understand what is happening. "Flora doesn't play anything."

I have never seen so much sadness as the look that comes over Flora's dad when he hears me say these words. He is crying. I don't know what to do. I don't think I have ever seen a grown man cry. I think he is crying because Flora does not play or because she doesn't speak to him. Because Flora once told me she did not understand why I would be sad that my father might die. My hand is reaching towards him to take back my recorder so I can say goodbye and leave this complicated man to his pain and this family to their mess.

The door beside me flies open and there in the door frame stands Flora. She moves towards us, her father's eyes streaming, and my hand outreached towards him.

And she is screaming.

Rabbia

rage

I have never seen Flora
Anything but calm

Apart from the few occasions
When her nostrils flare

Or jaw tightens
When anyone mentions

Her father.

Even in those moments
Before and after

She reached towards Shannon's
Extended hair

Flora looked, if anything,
Mildly surprised

To have
Found herself

In such an unusual
Predicament.

Standing in the door frame my friend
Has been replaced

By a siren.
Her hair is wild.

Her teeth are bared.
Her eyes are blazing.

As they from flick from me
To him.

From her friend
To her father.

And something is hanging in the air
Between us all

Something that wasn't
There before

Something that I need to grasp
Just out of reach.

Flora takes two steps forward
As if

She is going
To hit me.

To do what she did to Shannon
To me.

But a new version of Flora
Has taken over

The version that has replaced
My friend

Does not want to rip out
My hair.

Flora snatches my recorder
From his hand.

The recorder my father
Gave me.

The recorder that Flora has been
Encouraging me to play.

I'm not able to move
Or make a sound

As Flora's rage smashes
My recorder

Across the freshly installed
Marble counter

Fracturing it in
Two pieces.

There isn't enough time
In that moment

For me to consider how much fury
It would take

To crack a recorder that cost
One thousand euro.

How much pain would
Be needed

To damage a recorder made of
Castello boxwood

How much pain
A person would want to cause

To

F A R R U T E C

A recorder given to a friend
By her sick father.

Brisé

broken

Burrasca

music that imitates a storm

If she is appalled, sorry
Or horrified

I have no idea.

I am snatching the pieces of
My recorder

From her counter and
Floor.

Her father is speaking.
Is he yelling?

I run past Flora, her face returned
To that

Inexplicable
Calm.

How many times have I
Run home

Crying, in this last year
Of my life?

How many times have I burst
Through the door

Looking for comfort and greeted
By silence

Or sickness.
Or pain.

"Daisy?" My mother's voice is
Panicked

At the sound of me
Screaming.

"What happened?" My father is calling
From his chair

In the living room and
Tadgh and Fiachra

Are here as well and how have I
So offended

The gods that they insist I have
This entire audience

Here to witness this final moment
Of my deteriorating wall.

"I'm fine," I shout, doing my best
To push past my mother.

"You're not fine, Daisy.
What happened?"

"No," I scream, and I can see
All their faces

Are stricken at the sight
Of me.

At the sight of my pain.
At the sight of my rage.

"I can take care of
Myself.

That is what you all want
Isn't it?"

I drop the cracked recorder from
My hands and

All four sets of eyes move
From my livid face

To the sound of the wood
Hitting the tile

On the hallway floor and
As they fall

I make my way past my
Gaping family

Into salvation behind a locked
Bedroom door.

Heftig

violent, impetuous

No one comes to me
That night.

The next morning, my father calls me
To the kitchen.

My mother is sitting at the
Table.

The pieces of my new recorder
In her hands.

Tadgh and Fiachra
Across from her

Clearly unsure why they
Are here

My father takes his usual spot leaning
In the door frame

Thin, his eyes dark,
His skin grey.

His hair beginning
To thin.

He smiles at the broken
Recorder.

"Don't know what you have until
It's gone, eh?"

I crumble once again at the sight
Of those pieces.

And he moves
Towards me

He puts his arms around me
And shussshes.

He shouldn't be hugging me.
It isn't safe.

But I can't
Pull away.

As everything that has happened

To him.
To me.
To us.

Cascades out of me in an ocean
Of sobs.

And no one here tells me
To stop.

No one here tells me it
Doesn't matter.

No one here tells me I need to
Grow up.

My family are here all together
And for the first time

In a very long time they
Let me cry.

And something other
Than grief rumbles

From deep inside me and is
Tumbling out.

"Why didn't you make
Me practise?"

I am screaming into their
Astonished faces.

"This never would have happened if you
Made me practise.

Why didn't you tell me that I was letting
Myself

Get carried away
With David?

Where were you? Why didn't you
Stop it?"

The sobs that come from me are
About everything.

Everything that has happened
And

Everything that I have
Lost.

I understand now that music
Will not always save me

I understand now that friends
Will not always be there

I understand now that hearts
Will get broken

I understand now that my parents
Will not always

Be here to pick up the
Pieces.

Are they looking
At me?

Are they thinking how
Dare she?

This selfish girl who we asked nothing for
But happiness.

We wanted nothing for her
But joy.

We craved nothing for her
But contentment.

And in their time of crisis
When all they needed

Was that happy girl, here
I am.

Accusing them of being the one thing
They are not.

The one thing they have never been.
Bad parents.

The dam has broken.

They learn about David
And Shannon

The Christmas
Exam results

Ms Willis and
The Grade Five

The lack of practice
How worried I am

For my future.
For their future.

How worried I am that my father
Is going to die.

I tell them about all the things I search
At night

When everyone is
Asleep.

Statistics on survival rates
Statistics on recovery complications

My parents and brothers react
At all the right spots

Until I have nothing left
To say.

"Daisy." My father's voice is a shadow
Of what it was

And I am ready to hear
All the things

He has to say about how
I have disappointed them

All the things that I have done to make them
Less proud.

"Daisy."

"We didn't know what to do."

"We didn't want to push."

"We didn't know what to do."

"We worried we put you under too much pressure."

"We didn't want you to hate it."

"We didn't want you to hate us."

"We didn't know what to do."

"And the boys they took up."
"So much of our attention."
"Twins doing the Leaving Cert."
"And they both wanted to be doctors."
"And we overlooked it, Daisy."
"I am sorry, but we just didn't notice
At the start and by the time we did..."

I can see my brothers want
To react

To defend themselves against
This accusation.

With a wave from my father
They are silenced.

"It seemed like it was too late, and we didn't
Know what to do."
"We hoped you would find your way back."
"On your own."
"And we know that we have been expecting too much."
"Parents aren't given a manual
For this kind of thing."
"We did our best."
"And we can't reassure you
That everything is going to be okay."
"We hope it will be."
"And the doctors are positive."
"But we have no idea

Whether or not the treatment is working."
"We all just have to wait and see."
"Forgive us, Daisy, please."

They are the ones who are asking
For forgiveness.

And it is a joy and relief to
Give it to them.

Sturm und Drang

storm and stress

"Now," my father says an hour later
When we are all

Drinking tea and the twins have
Escaped the drama.

"What is all this about, do we think?"
He gestures towards

The broken pieces I still
Cannot look at.

"This is what I
Have heard,

I don't know how much of it
Is true."

My mother,
Is not a gossip.

She is not the kind of woman
Who takes joy

In sharing the news of other people's
Suffering.

She always said her world was
Too big,

Too bright, too free
Of pain,

To find the need to spread
Gossip about others.

"Flora's father was a lecturer,
In Trinity College.

One of the best. We knew him
From school

And that he was going to be
The one

That went places with his talents,
With his music."

She cocks her head
And looks at me.

"The only other person
I know who plays music

The way that he can
Is you.

There was something
Different about him."

She takes a moment,
And goes on.

"Everyone was an adult.
Everyone was consenting.

But a man should
Know better

Than to get entangled
With his student."

This is where Flora's rage
Has come from.

Her panic at her father's interest
In my recorder.

Even though
I know

He saw me only as his
Daughter's friend.

Perhaps his kindness towards me was one
Of the ways

He is trying to make up to his daughter
For his past.

"It's none of our business,"
My mother says,

"What happened before they
Came back here.

And none of this is Flora's fault.
Her father is not perfect.

No one's father is.
Not even yours, Daisy.

He is trying to make up for a mistake
He made.

He wanted a fresh start, we can all
Understand that.

I am not saying that what she has done
Is not terrible

To you.
And to us.

But I wonder what it looked like
To her

His lips on your recorder."

My father shifts at my
Mother's words.

"We can buy another
Recorder for you.

But I don't think you should close your heart
On Flora.

Just yet."

Commosso
moved

"Will you play it for us?"
My mother asks.

"Get your old recorder out. Play us
Something easy.

We can get some of your old teddy bears
If you would like?"

My father smiles, remembering
Those days

When I would make them part of my
Teddy concerts.

My heart lifts, this is what
I need

To go back to
The beginning

When music was blended with the
Love of performing

When perfection was an afterthought and all
That mattered was

Doing what I loved in front of
An audience

Of adoring fans and
Teddy bears.

"What would you like to hear?"
I ask.

"Anything at all," she says. I go
To my room

And dig around for that
Old recorder

That served me
So well.

Once they're gathered,
I take to the stage.

"This is called
'Three Blind Mice'."

Facile

easy

Alone again in my bedroom that night
I am searching

With hands that are steady, I type her name
Into YouTube

I only get as far as
Flora D

Before the suggested titles
Begin to fill

Flora Dunne plays...

I need to see every video.
Every performance.

She does not need the music
In front of her.

I can tell.

It is there for show.
To ensure

She does not seem too boastful
To her audience.

Her timing is perfect.
Her expression is perfect.
Her dynamics are perfect.

I watch those videos and remember
How

Her father spoke
About her.

About how she played.
How she moved.
How she performed.
How she was built for it.
Trained for it.
Born for it.

He did not do it
Justice.

Flora has not given up playing because
She cannot play.

She has not given up the piano because
She is traumatised.

Flora understands that no music
Is a punishment.

I was punishing myself, she saw it
Before I did.

Flora has given up the piano
To punish her father.

For the betrayal of her mother.
For the betrayal of their family.

For the humiliation.
For the pain.

Flora knows exactly how to hurt
Her father.

She took away her music.
And it kills her.

But Flora doesn't care
About herself

She hates
Her father.

Maybe that was why she couldn't stand
To see me

In pain, because I love
My father

And he loves me more than anything else
In the world.

And Flora's father may
Love her

More than anything else
In the world.

But for a time in his life he
Allowed himself

To forget, and Flora will never
Let him

Forget that
He forgot.

Cori spezzati

broken choirs, choirs in different places
singing in a stereo effect

Flora and I never
Existed.

At school she makes sure she is
Late to every class.

In choir she looks at her music
And not me.

Our Cantata performance is scheduled
The night after

The Music practical.

"Do you think she will apologise?"
My mother asks,

One night after she has collected me
From choir

Noticing Flora standing alone waiting
For her mother.

Flora does not admit when she
Is wrong.

I cannot say for sure that she believes
She is.

"It's possible to forgive her anyway,"
My mother says.

I am not sure I want to
Forgive Flora.

I want to focus

On me.
On my music.
On my family.

As my life moves further away from what
It was

And closer to what it will be after this
Final year of school.

Cantabile

singable, in a singing style

I practise
          and practise
                    and practise
                              and practise

I think about Flora and how her fingers danced
Across the piano keys

As if they were connected
To nothing

The way
She turned the pages of music
She didn't need.

I want to play like Flora
But

I need to play
Like me.

Not me then
Me now.

Play like something has changed.
Play like something has shifted.

Not for competition
Or ambitions or attention.

Play because I love it.
Because music is what I need.

To heal.
To grow.
To change.

Running order

the order in which songs or other items are presented at an event

Morning Practice
A series of scales and pieces in anticipation of an afternoon practical timeslot.

Performer: Daisy Ryan

Interruption for Apology
A performance of apologies for needing to go to Dublin on such an important day. Promises will be made about phone calls. Kisses will be given for

good luck. Requests will be made that legs should be broken.

Performers: Daisy's parents
Accompanied by Daisy Ryan

An Appointment
A performance where two nervous people in the audience will receive results to an earlier performed scan.

Performers: a consultant

Present at School
Students are expected to attend classes.

Performers: Daisy Ryan
and other classmates

A Phone Call
A presentation of results.

Performers: Daisy's parents
Accompanied by Daisy Ryan

Practical Performance
Bach and other pieces that have been neglected

Performer: Daisy Ryan and a
surprise mystery guest

Practical Performance
Six solo singing pieces

Performer: Flora Dunne

Intermission

Evening Performance
Bach 78 Cantata to be performed in front of local Leaving Certificate students and friends and family. Due to prior commitments, Daisy's parents will not be in attendance.

Performers: Daisy Ryan,
Flora Dunne and others

Cadence

two chords at the end of a piece which provide a type of punctuation at the end of a musical phrase

This is not the first time
I have

Been waiting for a phone
Call

Instead of practising for
An exam.

The phone is ringing.
The phone is ringing.

My mother is crying.

I don't want to hear what
She has to say

I do not want to hear what
She has to tell me.

But something breaks through the
Crying.

She is laughing.

“He is responding to the treatment
Well.

We still have a long way to go,
Daisy,

But he will be
Fine.

He is going to be fine,
Daisy.”

Prick-song

to prick is an obsolete English verb meaning to mark; this term was applied to music that was written down

I am pacing the hall listening
To the notes

Of the student before me.
It sounds like

It is going well
For her.

I am next. Flora is the last of
The day.

I know thanks to the schedule
Ms Willis

Emailed to us all. I wondered
Would she come

To wish me luck. A voice
Calls my name.

But it is not
Flora.

"Daisy."

David is here.

A familiar sight.
Unfamiliar.

He should be in

Another place.
Another time.

Another school.
Another world.

"Daisy." I cannot allow
His voice

To creep in
And block out

The notes I have been
Practising.

I need to keep them playing
In my head.

"I wanted to see would you
Think

About bringing me to the Debs
With you?"

There is a thundering in my
Ears.

The first thing that
Has replaced

The notes of Bach in my head
For weeks.

"It's just that it would
Be nice to go

And no one else will
Take me

Because they are angry about that
Stupid Curse."

He looks indignant, bewildered at
His former classmates'

Reluctance to take him to an
Event

After he disappointed
So many.

"We could have
A laugh

Spend the night with
My friends.

It could be good craic.
Think about it."

What could he possibly
Be thinking?

Did he know

Today would be the day of
My practical?

This morning, when he
Woke up

And decided to come here?
Today,

Now, of all the times,
Of all the days?

The day to wander back
Into this place

And ask me to take him to
The Debs?

"You want to come to
The Debs?"

He smirks at my
Confusion.

"They don't have one in
That place."

He jerks his head in a
Vague direction

Towards his new
School.

"It's something I should
Be allowed to do.

It isn't fair that I don't
Get to go."

Did he always have this much
Audacity?

There are a lot of things
I had

A right to do this
Year.

I had a right to be able to
Make mistakes

I had a right to go drinking
With friends

I had a right to play music
With joy

I had a right to sing
With abandon.

"You came here to ask me to take you
To the Debs?"

"Well, that and to empty
My locker.

To get back the hundred
Quid deposit."

To clean out his locker
To get his mother's money.

"I heard your practical was on.
I thought

I better catch you before
You went in."

Today.
Today.
Today.

It had to be
Today.

"You knew I had my practical?"
"Yeah, one of the lads told me."

"And you came here?"

"Well, it suited me, like, since I was
Here anyway."

I can't stop myself.
Not that I want to.

I remember my mother's
Words:

Say nothing.
Do nothing.
Keep going.

But I also remember some other words
She said recently.

"Fuck off, you selfish
Prick."

Fiero

proud, fierce, high spirited

He is taken aback.
Offended.

That I would speak to him
In this way.

That I would not jump
At the chance

To be with him
Again.

If only for
One night.

He does not have the grace
Or maturity

To look offended
For long.

He smirks
Raising one eyebrow

Not convinced
That I have no interest

In his proposal, blind
To the fact

That this is not the
First time

His actions have affected

My life.
My music.
My opportunities.

He must have known that today was
The day

That I have been
Preparing for.

He never even said, "I am sorry about
Your dad."

I don't think he chose this day
On purpose

To be malicious
Or cruel.

To make an appearance at
This school

Where he has not been since
His parents

Pulled him away from
His friends

And his sports
And me.

He knew it was important
To me

He just didn't
Care.

Because his life is more important
to him.

"Think about it," he says.
"No," I say.

"I've given you enough."

His smirk
Falters slightly.

I turn my back and walk
Towards my exam.

Ritenuto

an instruction to slow down and hold back

I am turning off
My phone

When I see a message
From Flora.

Bach loved the recorder.
Good luck.

That is all she has to say.
I will

Have to decide if that is
Enough for me

To forgive
That broken soul.

I owe something to
Flora

Who helped me find my way
Back.

Though I walked this
Path alone

She pointed me in the
Right direction.

This moment isn't about
Flora or David

It isn't even about a final
Exam

It is about something bigger
And smaller

It's about my music
And me.

Fine
end

I am doing my best
To keep focus

On the pieces that I need
To perform

Running over and over
In my head

The parts that always
Give me trouble.

"Do your best,"
My mother said this morning

As she and my father
Gathered up the things

They would need for his last
Chemo treatment.

Radiation will be in
A few weeks.

Before leaving she held me for
A long time.

I could feel all
The things

She was trying
to say.

That she knew they should
Be there.

But they couldn't miss this last
appointment

Scheduled to begin at
The exact time

I would be picking up
My music.

David and Flora

Are fighting for my
Attention

As I push open
The door.

My old recorder
Familiar and

Tight in my hand
Cold wood

Against a hot
Palm.

I step into the
Classroom

And approach the examiner
Who smiles.

New words come into my
Mind

As I place my music onto
Its stand

And make some unnecessary
Adjustments.

He's going to be fine.
He's going to be fine.
He's going to be fine.

I don't need to think about David.
Or Shannon.
Or Flora.

I need to think about
Bach.

About his life
And his music.

About my life
And my music.

About my brothers.
About my mother.

About my father.
Sitting

In that hospital
Room.

That poison being streamed
Into him.

For the last time.

"I see you have picked some
very ambitious pieces.

I have always loved this
From the Partita.

Would you like to start
with that?"

I nod. I do want to start with
Bach.

I am calm.

"Take all the time you need to tune
And get comfortable."

I check the clock.

My father will be
In that chair.

The slow drip of the clear
liquid

Filling his blood.

He's going to be fine.
He's going to be fine.
He's going to be fine.

I bring the recorder to
my lips.

I give it three smooth
Blows.

I nod. She nods.

"You can start when
You're ready."

We hope you have enjoyed reading *Solo*. On the following pages you will find out about some other Little Island books you might like to read next.

THINGS I KNOW

by Helena Close

Things I know. I'm a bad person.
I miss Finn. I could easily be a murderer.

Saoirse can't wait to leave school – but just before the Leaving Cert her ex-boyfriend dies by suicide. Everyone blames Saoirse, and her rumbling anxieties spiral out of control.

Saoirse feels herself flailing in swirling waters that threaten to suck her into the depths. No-one can save her – not her lovely nan; not the gorgeous boy who tries hard to love her; not her fabulous best friend; and certainly not her cheap-wisdom counsellor.

Can Saoirse, against all odds, rescue the self she used to know?

'Read it – and buy a second copy to thrust into the hands of the next platitude-utterer you encounter.'
The Irish Times

'An accurate portrayal of a young person's challenges, this book is also full of hope, love and laughter.'
The Sunday Independent

Also from Little Island Books

THE GONE BOOK

by Helena Close

I know you'll hate me. I just know you will. But I can't help it. I'm going to find you.

Matt's mam left home when he was 10. He writes letters to her but doesn't send them. He keeps them in his Gone Book, which he hides in his room. Fivc years of letters about his life. Five years of hurt.

Matt's dad won't talk about her. His older brother is mixed up with drugs and messing with dangerous characters. His friends, Mikey and Anna, are the best thing in his life, but Matt keeps pushing them away.

All Matt wants to do is skate, surf, and forget. But now his mam is back in town and Matt knows he needs to find her, to finally deliver the truth.

Praise for *The Gone Book*

"Dark and gritty and desperately sad and wildly funny, this is as real as writing gets"
– Donal Ryan

"A skillful and truthful novel from a wonderful storyteller"
– Joseph O'Connor

"I would highly recommend this book"
– *Paper Lanterns*

Awards

Winner of the White Raven Award 2021

Nominated for the Yoto Carnegie Medal for Writing 2021

Shortlisted for the An Post Irish Book Awards: Dept 51 @ Eason Teen and Young Adult Book of the Year 2020

Shortlisted for the Biennial Literacy Association of Ireland Young Adult Book Award 2021

Also from Little Island Books

THE ETERNAL RETURN OF CLARA HART

by Louise Finch

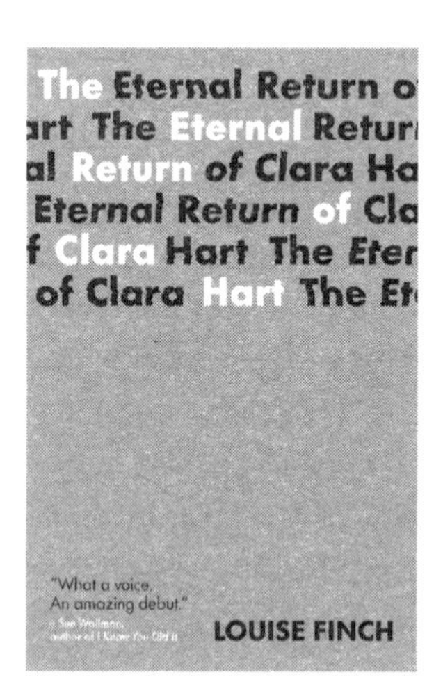

A sensational YA debut about toxic masculinity and gendered violence

Wake up. Friday. Clara Hart hits my car. Go to class. Anthony rates the girls. House party. Anthony goes upstairs with Clara. Drink. Clara dies. Wake up. Friday again. Clara Hart hits my car. Why can't I break this loop?

A flicker in the fabric of time gives Spence a second chance. And a third. How many times will he watch the same girl die?

Praise for *The Eternal Return of Clara Hart*

"Compulsively readable"
– *The Guardian*

"I am glad this superb book exists"
– *The Irish Times*

"A devastating, essential journey"
– *Kirkus*, starred review

"Bold and honest"
– *The National*

Awards

Shortlisted for the Yoto Carnegie Medal for Writing 2023

Shortlisted for the Branford Boase Award 2023

Shortlisted for the Great Reads Award 2023

Shortlisted for the Badger Book Award 2023

Shortlisted for the YA Book Prize 2023

Also from Little Island Books

TRIGGER

by C.G. Moore

An unflinching verse novel about a teenage boy who struggles to come to terms with his own sexual assault

Jay wakes in a park, beaten and bruised. He can't remember what happened the night before. But he has suspicions.

Jay realises he has been raped — and that his ex-boyfriend may have been involved.

Counselling sessions cause Jay to question everything. His new friend Rain encourages his pursuit of justice. Jay wants answers, but his search will lead him down a perilous path.

Praise for *Trigger*

"Pulls no punches in its exploration of consent and self-acceptance"
– *Irish Examiner*

"An important book which I am sure will help many readers feel seen and less alone"
– Waterstones Bookseller Review

"An uncomfortable read but it is absolutely a story worth reading"
– *Paper Lanterns*

Awards

Nominated for the Yoto Carnegie Medal for Writing 2025

Selected for the Kirkus Best Teen & YA Verse Novels 2025

Also from Little Island Books

GRAPEFRUIT MOON

by Shirley-Anne McMillan

How far would you go to fit in?

Wealthy, popular Charlotte and quiet Drew from the council estate don't have much in common. Except for Adam — Charlotte's ex and leader of the toxic Stewards club.

As Drew struggles to follow the Stewards' rules, Adam is terrorising Charlotte with a video of them having sex.

A trip to Spain, poetry slams and a drag queen bring Charlotte and Drew closer together — and push them further than ever from who they used to be.

Praise for *Grapefruit Moon*

"Emotional, gripping, and so, so real"
– Louise Finch, author of *The Eternal Return of Clara Hart*

"A delicate and candid depiction of two teens' efforts to shape their uncertain futures while navigating weighty issues"
– *Publishers Weekly*

"McMillan's latest is a raw, honest work with nuanced characterization set in a Belfast private school"
– *Kirkus*, starred review

Acknowledgement

recognition of the importance or quality of something

It's an incredibly humbling experience sitting down to write a list of people to thank and realising just how many people in your life have gotten you and your book to this point. First, my deepest gratitude to my agent, Sallyanne Sweeney, for believing in this project from its inception, and to Niamh Mulvey for her faith and generosity.

Thank you to The Arts Council of Ireland and the Agility Award, which eased a lot of pressure during the writing of this novel.

Alex Dunne, for being my first reader, friend and confidant. I am grateful to my early readers, particularly Sadhbh Kenny, Elena Browne, Dean Kelly and Méadbh McDonnell, who not only reassured me this could be something special but also offered direction and notes in the kind and generous ways delicate egos need to hear them.

Cecelia Madden, my choir director, for providing the space that brought music back into my life and ensured the musical accuracy of Daisy's experience. Thank you also to the creators of the *Oxford Dictionary of Music Terms*. Any errors are mine alone.

I owe my writing career to the MA in Creative Writing programme at the University of Limerick. Joseph O'Connor, Donal Ryan and Martin Dyar provided guidance and encouragement, treating me as a creative equal. They remain wonderful champions and friends. Sarah Moore Fitzgerald deserves special mention for her support that extends far beyond that year in UL. Our time together is always creatively restorative and balm for the soul. My writing groups, Writepace and Silver Apples, particularly Dan, Sarah, Katheryn and Claire, for helping build a space full of laughter and creativity during those dark lockdown days.

Elana McKernan for her guidance and insight that arrived at the exact moment Daisy and Flora did. Without her, this book may never have been finished. The supportive friends that I worked alongside in O'Mahony's for so many years, and the new friends I have made since joining the team of Kennys. Particularly thanks to Colette Cotter for teaching me everything there is to know about the book trade.

Ireland's booksellers are tireless champions of literature, and I am grateful for their work, friendship and support. Thanks to Cian Byrne and Sarah and Tomás Kenny for their extra support. The entire team at Little Island. It has been a pleasure to work with you all – thank you for how kindly you have treated me and Daisy on our journey to get this book on the shelves.

My parents, Mary and Paul, for teaching me to read, encouraging me to write, and for supporting my fictionalising a time in our lives that was tricky, scary and painful. My brothers, Ronan and Cian, sisters-in-law Aoife and Máiread, for many things but mostly for bringing my favourite people into the world. Róisín, Máire, Darragh and Beíbhínn have taught me how much love I am capable of.

Finally, to my husband, T.J., thank you for bringing calm and joy into my life and for loving both me and this book. Every twist in my life has been worth it, because they all led me to you.

About the Author

Gráinne O'Brien is a bestselling author and a bookseller at Kennys, Galway, Ireland. She was a member of the Irish Booksellers Association committee and was named a Bookshop Hero by *The Bookseller* in 2022. She is the founder of Rontu Literary Service, an agency dedicated to supporting writers of fiction for children as they seek publication. She completed the MA in Creative Writing from the University of Limerick in 2018 and received Arts Council Agility Awards in 2021, 2022 and 2023. Her picturebook *A Limerick Fairytale* was published by The O'Brien Press in 2023. *Solo* is her first novel.

ABOUT LITTLE ISLAND

Little Island is an award-winning independent Irish publisher of books for young readers, founded in 2010 by Ireland's first Laureate na nÓg (children's laureate), Siobhán Parkinson. Little Island books are found throughout Ireland, the UK, North America, and in translation around the world.

You can find out more at littleisland.ie

RECENT AWARDS FOR LITTLE ISLAND

Highly Commended: British Book Awards Small Press of the Year 2024; Youth Libraries Group (UK) Publisher of the Year 2023

IBBY Honour List 2024

The Táin by Alan Titley, illus. by Eoin Coveney

Things I Know by Helena Close

An Post Irish Book Awards: Teen and YA Book of the Year 2023; Shortlisted: British Book Awards 2024

Black and Irish: Legends, Trailblazers & Everyday Heroes by Leon Diop and Briana Fitzsimons, illus. by Jessica Louis

An Post Irish Book Awards: Children's Book of the Year (Senior) 2023

I Am the Wind: Irish Poems for Children Everywhere ed. by Sarah Webb and Lucinda Jacob, illus. by Ashwin Chacko

White Raven Award 2023; Shortlisted: Carnegie Medal for Writing 2023; Shortlisted: YA Book Prize 2023; Finalist: Kirkus Prize 2023

The Eternal Return of Clara Hart by Louise Finch